The Case of the Rising Stars

"We're filming a shoot-out scene," the director explained to the spectators. "But don't worry, the bullets are blanks."

Someone yelled, "Action!" Dan Redding, the show's handsome star, jumped up and fired his gun toward the "criminal" crouching in the doorway of a building to Nancy's right.

Nancy heard a clang. She looked up and saw a bullet hole in a No Parking sign above her head!

Nancy turned back to tell Redding his gun was loaded with real bullets, not blanks. Then she saw him whirl around and point the gun directly at her.

Wait! Nancy wanted to scream, but the word froze in her throat.

Redding pulled the trigger and fired again.

Nancy Drew Mystery Stories

Available from MINSTREL Books

NANCY DREW®

THE CASE OF
THE RISING STARS

CAROLYN KEENE

A MINSTREL® BOOK

PUBLISHED BY POCKET BOOKS

New York · London · Toronto · Sydney · Tokyo

A MINSTREL PAPERBACK *ORIGINAL*

 A Minstrel Book, published by
POCKET BOOKS, a division of Simon & Schuster Inc.
1230 Avenue of the Americas, New York, NY 10020

Copyright © 1989 by Simon & Schuster Inc.
Cover art copyright © 1989 Linda Thomas
Produced by Mega-Books of New York, Inc.

ISBN: 0-671-66312-7

First Minstrel Books printing February 1989

10 9 8 7 6 5 4 3 2 1

Contents

1

Kidnapped

The detective flung open the heavy brass doors
and strode into the lobby of Chicago's Buckingham Hotel. Nancy Drew, standing in the check-in
line with Bess Marvin and George Fayne, could
tell he was a detective. He was making it so
obvious. He wore a trench coat and a felt hat, just
like a detective in an old-fashioned movie mystery. He also had an enormous magnifying glass
dangling from a chain around his neck.

The doors slammed shut behind the detective.
Overhead, the chandelier quivered ominously. A
hush settled over the crowded room.

"There has been a murder," the detective said
quietly. His voice drifted through the elegant

wood-paneled hall. "And every one of you is a suspect."

"The butler did it!" shouted a teenage boy. Everybody laughed.

The detective laughed too. He was a tall young man who looked to be in his early twenties. He unbuttoned his trench coat. Underneath, he wore faded jeans and a T-shirt that said, "Everybody Loves a Mystery Lover." Then he stood at the end of the check-in line behind Nancy, Bess, and George.

"That was pretty funny," said blond, blue-eyed Bess, turning to the young man.

"Just trying to liven things up," he said. "All this waiting is really boring. Last year's convention was much better organized. This your first time at a Mystery Lovers Convention?"

The girls nodded.

"I guess you're not too familiar with mysteries, then."

Nancy and her friends shared a private look. The young man obviously didn't know that Nancy Drew was a famous detective from River Heights. At the age of eighteen she had already solved mysteries all over the world. Nancy never liked to brag, though. All she said was, "I'll bet you've been to a lot of these conventions."

"Five," he said.

Nancy tucked her reddish blond hair behind

her ear and fixed her keen blue eyes on the young man. "And I'll bet you're about to tell us everything we need to know."

"Excellent deduction." He laughed. "They've got all kinds of exhibits. Mystery books, TV shows, movies, you name it. And did you hear who the special guest stars are? Will Leonard and Sally Belmont, the stars of 'Nightside.'"

"Nightside," the number-one show on TV, was a mystery series about a happy-go-lucky newlywed couple who ran a private detective agency. It was actually more of a romantic comedy than a mystery. The couple was always joking around, even when their lives were in danger.

"'Nightside' is my favorite show," said George, a tall, slim girl with short curly brown hair and brown eyes. George was Bess's first cousin, and the two of them were Nancy Drew's best friends.

"And Will Leonard is my favorite star." Bess sighed. "He's so cute. I just love his shaggy hair and blue eyes, and the way his clothes always look slept in."

"I read somewhere that he's only five-foot-seven," George said. "That's too short. I like my TV stars *tall*."

"Well, Sally's more my speed," said the young man. "She's got class. I'm going to try to meet her later. They're signing autographs at two o'clock."

"Then that's where *I'll* be at two o'clock," Bess

said. "Just think of the possibilities. I'll lend Will my pen . . . he'll sign his name . . . then, as he's handing the pen back to me, our eyes will meet, the sparks will fly, and—"

"Next," called the hotel clerk.

"I think you're in the wrong place," said Nancy as the girls moved up to the counter to register. "You want the *Romance* Lovers Convention."

After checking into their room, Nancy made a quick call to River Heights. She wanted to let the Drews' housekeeper, Hannah Gruen, know that they had arrived safely in Chicago. Hannah had taken care of Nancy and her father, Carson Drew, for fifteen years, ever since Nancy's mother had died. Nancy loved Hannah and knew the housekeeper would worry if she didn't call.

After Nancy got off the phone, the girls took the elevator down to the Grand Ballroom. The elevator doors opened onto a reception area. Beyond it was a huge room divided by rows of booths. The aisles were crowded with people of every age and description, jostling one another for a better view of the exhibits.

At the far end of the room was a stage. A banner hanging over it read "Welcome Mystery Lovers of America."

"Hey, look," said George, suddenly pointing to a booth that was several feet away. "Do you know who that is?"

4

Nancy and Bess stood on tiptoe to see who George was talking about.

A sign above a booth said "Multi Press of New York." A tall, heavyset middle-aged woman with dyed blond hair sat at the booth. She was wearing bifocal glasses and a red hooded sweatshirt with a logo that said "I'm a Fifi Fan." In front of her were stacks and stacks of brand-new hardcover books.

Dozens of people were lined up in front of the booth as she signed the inside cover of each book.

"That's Eileen Braddock, the mystery author," said George. "I bet she's autographing *The Dark Side of Danger*. That's her latest book."

"I know you're a fan of hers," Nancy remarked.

George nodded, her eyes sparkling with excitement. "I've read every one of her books. All twenty-seven of them. The most famous one was *Death by Fear*. Bess read it, too."

"Right," said Bess, shivering. "It was so scary I would only let myself read it in the mornings so I wouldn't stay up all night."

"Why does her sweatshirt say 'I'm a Fifi Fan'?" Nancy asked.

"That's for the detective she's put in her last few novels," George said. "Fifi Spinelli. She's really young and beautiful with long blond hair, and when she's not solving crimes, she's an aerobics instructor."

"And she has all these really great clothes," Bess added. "Designer outfits from Paris."

"Just what *all* young detectives are wearing this year," Nancy joked, striking a model's pose in her jeans and denim jacket.

The next display they came to was set up to look like an English parlor. Posed around high-backed leather armchairs and a Persian rug were actors dressed as a butler, an English colonel, an elderly aristocratic woman, and a French maid. A man, dressed in a tuxedo, lay facedown on the rug with a knife sticking out of his back. A large freestanding sign at the front of the scene advertised a new board game called "Whodunit?"

"Maybe this time the butler *did* do it," whispered George.

Suddenly the girls were pushed roughly from behind. Bright lights started flashing over their heads, and they were forced to move to one side as two people were escorted through the crowd.

"Who is it?" asked Bess. "Can anybody see?"

"It's two o'clock," said Nancy, checking her watch. "My guess is that it's Will Leonard and Sally Belmont. We'd better get over to the stage if you want to get Will Leonard's autograph."

Bess groaned. "How will we ever get through all these people? I can't even breathe."

Nancy grabbed Bess's hand. "I've got an idea. Follow me." Nancy pulled Bess into the English parlor. "Excuse us," she said as she stepped lightly over the dead body and headed for the narrow passageway between the backs of the booths.

"Wait for me," said George, following.

Threading their way between the booths, the girls made much better time than the other conventioneers stuck in the aisles. They arrived just as a line was beginning to form at the foot of the steps leading up to the stage.

Onstage, the two stars sat down behind a long table. A young woman staggered in under several cardboard boxes. She opened the boxes and pulled out large glossy black-and-white photographs of Will and Sally.

The line started to move forward.

"Oh, no!" Bess said in a panicky voice. "I haven't figured out yet what I'm going to say to him."

"How about 'hello'?" said Nancy. "That ought to work."

"Or 'I like your show,'" suggested George.

"That's so *boring*," Bess moaned. "This is my big chance to make an impression. I need to sound *sophisticated*."

"Guess you'll have to come up with something off the top of your head," said Nancy. "And you'd better think fast. It's your turn."

Slowly, Bess approached her idol.

Will Leonard was a handsome man in his early thirties, with shaggy blond hair and a few days' growth of beard. With his black jeans, black sweatshirt, and sunglasses, he looked more like a rock star than a TV detective. He looked exactly as he did on TV—only he wasn't his usual smiling self.

"Mr. Leonard . . ." Bess began, but the TV star was deep in the middle of an argument with Sally Belmont.

"Don't tell me you had nothing to do with it," Will said, scowling. "You had your manager book you into this hotel weeks before I even knew about it, just so you could get the Presidential Suite. How many rooms did you get? Five?"

"Four," said Sally. "But it's not my fault if *your* manager isn't doing his job. Peter knew about this the same time Denise did, and he didn't make your reservations till last week."

"What Peter Thornton does is none of your business," said Will.

"What happened to the happy-go-lucky newlyweds of 'Nightside'?" Nancy whispered to Bess and George.

"Sounds like the honeymoon's over," George whispered back.

"They're not really married," Bess reminded her friends. "Those are just their roles in the show."

Sensing a pause in the argument, Bess said, "Mr. Leonard . . ."

Will Leonard looked up. "Yeah?" he said sourly.

Bess caught her breath. "Uh . . . hello. I like your show."

Without answering, Will took a photograph of Sally and himself off the top of the pile and scrawled his name. He shoved it across the table at Bess.

"Would it be too much trouble to ask you for a special dedication?" asked Bess.

"The only thing I'm dedicated to is getting this stupid thing over with," said Will. "Who's next?" he called, looking over Bess's shoulder.

Nancy put an arm around Bess's shoulder. "I am," she said, looking Will Leonard straight in the eye. "But after the way you talked to my friend, I don't *want* your autograph."

"Me neither," said George. The three girls started to walk away.

"Wait a minute," Sally Belmont called after them. The girls turned around. The beautiful star was looking at them with her famous blue eyes. In person they were even bluer than on TV. Her long black hair was draped over one shoulder like a band of satin.

"I'd like to apologize for my co-star's rudeness," said Sally. "We've both been under a lot of pressure lately. Getting to this convention has been nothing but one foul-up after another."

9

"Foul-ups for *me,* you mean," Will fumed. "Wait till I get my hands on Peter Thornton. He's dead meat."

"Will, calm down," said Sally, taking another picture from the pile. "What's your name, hon?" she asked Bess.

"Bess Marvin."

"Well, Bess, is there anything special you'd like me to write?"

Bess shrugged. "I don't care," she said. Nancy could tell her friend was still upset.

Sally spent a full minute writing, then handed the photograph to Bess.

"Thanks," Bess said without enthusiasm, starting to walk away with Nancy and George.

"Wait," Sally said. "I can't let three of our fans leave feeling so badly about the show. Tell you what. Why don't you three come up to my room later this afternoon for a visit?"

"Oh, brother." Will rolled his eyes. "Why don't you invite the whole convention? I'm sure there's room for *everybody* in the Presidential Suite."

"Ignore him," said Sally. "Let's say, four o'clock? Room Twelve-oh-four." She smiled warmly at the girls.

Bess's eyes opened wide. "You want us to come to your *room?*"

"Unless you have other plans," Sally said.

"Other plans . . ." Bess repeated, disbelievingly. She turned to George and Nancy. "Sally Belmont invites us to her room and she thinks I've got something *better* to do?"

Bess turned back to Sally and gave her a big grin. "We'll be there."

Two hours later the girls stood in the quiet, carpeted hallway outside Sally Belmont's room. Nancy knocked on the door.

"I can't believe she actually invited us up here," said Bess. "It almost makes me happy Will Leonard turned out to be such a jerk."

There was no answer, so Nancy knocked again and the door opened slightly. Pushing the door in farther, Nancy peered into the brightly lit marble foyer.

"Hello?" Nancy called, but there was no answer. "Ms. Belmont?" Nancy called in a louder voice.

There was still no answer.

Nancy stepped into the room. Bess and George followed her inside.

"Look at that," Nancy said, pointing to the floor. Two thin black skid marks cut two curving lines across the marble surface.

Nancy looked up. Straight ahead, at the end of the hall, was a living room. There were two bedrooms facing each other across the hall. Nancy noticed that the door to one of the bedrooms was hanging at a crazy angle. Nancy hurried to

11

the bedroom. All the dresser drawers had been dumped on the floor, clothes were everywhere, and chairs and tables were overturned.

Bess and George joined Nancy in the doorway. "What a mess!" Bess exclaimed. "What happened?"

"That's what I'd like to know," Nancy replied grimly.

Then she spotted a piece of paper pinned to the center of the bedspread. She picked her way through the mess and unpinned the note.

"What does it say?" asked George.

Nancy read the note aloud:

Sally's gone from 'Nightside' to an even darker side—and there's no escape. Watch the rerun as history repeats itself.

"What does it mean?" asked Bess, with a shudder.

"It means," said Nancy in a low voice, "that our star's been kidnapped!"

2

An Important Clue

"History will repeat itself?" George asked. "I don't get it."

"Neither do I," said Nancy. "But it looks like we're getting even more mystery this weekend than we bargained for. We'd better call hotel security."

Nancy burrowed through the clothing on the floor until she found the phone cord. Pulling it, she dragged the phone out from underneath the bed. Quickly she dialed the hotel operator.

"I'd like to speak to the chief of security, please," Nancy said. A few seconds later a raspy voice came on the line. "Hello?"

"Yes, hello. My name is Nancy Drew and I'm in Sally Belmont's room, Suite Twelve-oh-four. One of the bedrooms has been ransacked, and we've found a note saying she's been kidnapped."

Nancy listened a while, then said, "No, this isn't a joke . . . Yes, I realize there's a Mystery Lovers Convention going on . . . No, I don't know how many phone calls like this you get every year at this time . . ."

Nancy shot Bess and George a look that said, "The guy on the other end of this phone has a serious problem."

"Listen," Nancy said, beginning to lose her patience. "This is for real. Come see for yourself. Suite Twelve-oh-four." Nancy banged the phone down.

"Is someone coming?" Bess asked.

Nancy shrugged. "I hope so. Meanwhile, let's look for clues. I'll check in here. Why don't you two spread out over the other rooms."

Nancy glanced at Sally Belmont's clothes lying on the floor. Even though she was alarmed by the star's disappearance, Nancy couldn't help marveling at how expensive everything looked.

It must be nice to be a rich, famous TV star, thought Nancy. To have the biggest hotel rooms and expensive clothes and fans hounding you for your autograph. Then Nancy reminded herself that it *wouldn't* be nice to be Sally Belmont right now. At this moment Sally was probably tied up in some dark, scary place, and her life was in danger!

14

Nancy moved into the master bathroom. The bathroom was huge, almost as large as Nancy's bedroom at home. The walls and floor were covered with white porcelain tile.

"I know what Hannah would say," thought Nancy. "She'd say a white bathroom is impossible to keep clean because every speck of dust shows. But dust can show footprints and handprints."

Nancy checked the floor for dust, but it was sparkling clean—except for a small blue dot underneath the sink. Nancy stooped down to see what it was. It was round and made of clear blue plastic.

"It's a contact lens," Nancy said aloud. "So *that's* the secret behind those famous blue eyes— unless the contact lens belongs to the kidnapper."

Nancy took a glass of the bathroom shelf, removed the sanitized wrapper, and very carefully placed the lens inside the glass. Then she covered the glass again with the wrapper, and sealed the whole thing tight with a hair elastic lying on the edge of the sink.

George appeared in the bathroom doorway. "I found something," she said excitedly.

"So did I," Nancy said, showing George the contact lens in the glass.

"Do you think it belongs to the kidnapper?" George asked.

"That's what I want to figure out." Nancy tucked the glass inside her oversized purse. "What did you find?"

George held out a hardcover book titled *The Repeating Gunshot.* It was written by Eileen Braddock, the famous mystery writer the girls had seen earlier.

"Look inside the front cover," said George.

Nancy opened the book. The first page had a handwritten inscription:

To Sally—
Thanks for trying. Too bad it didn't work out.
—Eileen

"Sounds like they know each other," said George, looking over Nancy's shoulder.

"It sure does," Nancy said. "I wonder what Eileen Braddock was talking about," she added thoughtfully. "*What* didn't work out?"

George flipped to the first page of the story. "*The Repeating Gunshot* was such a great book," she said. "Did you ever read it?"

Nancy shook her head. "I've never read any of them."

"I've read all twenty-seven," said George.

"I know, you told me," Nancy said, smiling. "And you love that detective, Fifi Spaghetti—"

"Spinelli," George corrected her.

Nancy wasn't listening. She was deep in

thought. The book's inscription seemed friendly enough. But there was the possibility that it referred to something bad that happened between Eileen Braddock and Sally Belmont.

Braddock had written twenty-seven mysteries. One or more of those mysteries probably contained a kidnapping. Had the author set up a real-life kidnapping? Maybe she was mad about something and was seeking revenge. But for what? The title of the book was *The Repeating Gunshot.* The kidnapper's note had said history would repeat itself. Was there some connection?

"What's this book about?" Nancy asked George.

"It's really scary," George said. "This young English woman is kidnapped and taken to an old, decrepit mansion in the countryside. She thinks she's going crazy because she keeps hearing this gunshot over and over, but there's no gun and no one there to shoot it. Fifi saves her and solves the mystery, though, in the end."

"Interesting," said Nancy. "Let's hold on to this book."

The girls headed back into the foyer and ran into Bess.

"Find anything?" Nancy asked.

Bess shook her head. "Looks like no one went into the other rooms. There's even one of those 'Welcome to the Hotel' fruit baskets on the dining-room table that nobody touched."

"Except you," Nancy said, motioning toward the apple core in Bess's hand.

"It's only sixty calories," Bess said, smiling sheepishly. "It's definitely allowed on my new diet." Bess was slightly plump, and she was always on a diet. George said this was because Bess was always thinking about food.

There was a knock at the door. Nancy went to open it. A huge, bearlike man with watery blue eyes and a full head of white hair stood at the door. He wore a gray uniform with a patch on the shoulder that said "Buckingham Hotel Security," and he was smoking a fat cigar.

"You're not Sally Belmont," the man said, puffing on his cigar.

Nancy recognized his raspy voice. He was the security guard she had spoken to on the phone earlier. "Of course I'm not," said Nancy in an exasperated tone. "She's been kidnapped."

The security guard shook his head and exhaled a cloud of smoke. "You crazy mystery people! You're all alike. You get caught up in this mystery thing, and it's *me* who gets stuck riding up and down the elevators investigating one false alarm after another." He started to walk away, but Nancy grabbed his arm.

"Please come in," she said. "It will take us only a minute to prove to you that we're not lying. Just look in the bedroom."

18

Reluctantly, the security guard allowed himself to be led into the suite.

"I'm Nancy Drew, the girl who called," Nancy introduced herself. "And these are my friends, Bess Marvin and George Fayne."

"Ray Sherbinski," the man said. "Chief of security. Okay, junior detective, which way?"

Nancy pointed to the door dangling off its hinges. Sherbinski walked into the master bedroom and surveyed the damage. Then, without a word, he turned around and headed for the front door.

"Well?" Nancy asked. "Aren't you going to do anything?"

Sherbinski pulled a folded piece of paper out of his breast pocket and handed it to Nancy. Nancy read it.

"You see?" said Sherbinski, taking short puffs on his cigar. "It's exactly what I was expecting."

"I'm missing something," said Bess. "What's he talking about?"

"This memo is addressed to Mr. Sherbinski," said Nancy. "It says that a fake mystery will be staged today as part of the convention."

"And this is it," said Sherbinski. "So much for your kidnapping."

"Then where's Sally Belmont?" George asked. "She's still missing."

"She'll show up," Sherbinski replied.

"But she said she'd meet us here," Bess insisted. "Why would she tell us that if she knew she wasn't going to be here?"

"She probably set you up to discover the false crime. *Somebody* had to do it. Now, if you'll excuse me, I've got *real* business to attend to." Ray Sherbinski stepped out of the suite and shut the door firmly behind him.

"I don't buy it," said Nancy. "Maybe someone really did send him that memo, but I'm convinced this kidnapping is real."

"What do we do now?" George asked.

"We'll just have to find Sally Belmont ourselves," Nancy replied. "Come on."

As Bess and George followed Nancy out the front door, they saw Will Leonard letting himself into the room next door. He was still wearing his sunglasses.

"Mr. Leonard," Nancy called. "Can we speak to you, please?"

Will Leonard turned his back on them. "Autograph time is over," he said shortly.

"We didn't want your autograph before, and we don't want it now," Nancy said.

At this Will Leonard turned around. "Excuse me?" he said. Then he recognized them. "Oh, I remember you. You're the girls who got the special treatment from Sweet Sally. So? Did Madam President give you a tour of the Presidential Suite?"

"No, she didn't," Nancy said. "Because she's been kidnapped."

Will Leonard was unimpressed. "We've both been kidnapped at least half a dozen times," he said with a shrug. "Didn't you see last week's episode, 'The Sands of Time'?"

"We're not talking about the show," Bess said. "Sally Belmont's been kidnapped for real."

"We found this pinned to her bedspread," Nancy said, handing him the note.

Will Leonard took the note and read it. "You can come in for a *minute,*" he said finally, opening the door to his room. "But if you tell anybody else my room number, I'll have you kicked out of this hotel so fast the mystery will be why you ever came."

"What a charming invitation," Bess said sarcastically. "We'd love to."

The girls followed Will Leonard into his room. It was large and comfortable, but it was only one room, not an impressive suite like Sally's. Will flopped down into an easy chair. He didn't invite the girls to sit down, so they remained standing.

"The security chief said he got a memo saying a fake mystery would be set up as part of the convention. He's convinced Sally's disappearance was the fake mystery," Nancy said. "What do *you* think?"

"I agree," Will said. "Sally's always trying to be the center of attention. It wouldn't surprise me one bit if she set this whole thing up herself just to prove she's the *real* star of 'Nightside.' I think she's jealous because I get more fan mail than she does."

There was a knock at the door.

"See what I mean?" Will said. "My fans have already tracked me down. But I've seen enough fans for one day. Whoever you are—get lost!" he shouted.

The knocking became louder and more insistent.

"Don't you think you'd better answer that?" said Nancy.

Will shrugged. He stood up slowly, walked to the door, and opened it.

No one was there. Will stepped outside and looked up and down the hallway, but it was empty. "I don't get it," he said. Then he noticed that something was written on the front of the door. He took off his sunglasses to get a better look.

"What's the matter?" Nancy asked.

"This dumb stunt has gone too far," the TV star muttered.

The girls crowded around him.

Spray painted on the door, in bloodred letters, were two words: "You're next!"

3

The Plot Thickens

"You see?" Bess said shakily. "It wasn't a setup. And now they're coming after you, too!"

Will shut the door and flopped back down on the chair. "A little spray paint doesn't make it real. Sally's probably doing it to bring even more attention to her stupid practical joke. Well, sorry, Sally. Your plan's about to backfire."

Will reached for the phone and dialed the hotel operator. "Get me hotel security," he said.

"Wait!" Nancy cried.

"Who's this?" Will asked into the phone. "Ray Sherbinski? Say hey, Ray, this is Will Leonard in Room Twelve-oh-three . . ."

Nancy waved her arms to get Will's attention, but he ignored her.

"Yes, this is the *real* Will Leonard. Don't I sound like him? Anyway, I'd like to make a complaint about Sally Belmont. She just spray-painted my door. Yeah, it's all part of a publicity stunt. Anyway, I thought you might like to know since she defaced hotel property. Great. See you in a few."

Will hung up the phone. "We'll see how Sally likes *this* publicity," he said. "This is gonna look great in the *National Tattler.* BELMONT SEES RED OVER LEONARD'S SUCCESS." He smiled. "That was a really good headline, if I do say so myself. Don't you think so?"

The girls didn't say anything. They just stood there glumly. Barely two minutes later there was a knock on the door. Will opened it to a puff of cigar smoke and Ray Sherbinski.

"Hey, it really *is* you," said Sherbinski, breaking into a big smile. "This is the first honest call I've gotten all day. My wife watches your show every Tuesday night. You think I can get her your autograph? It would be the thrill of her life."

Will took a signed photograph off his dresser and handed it to Sherbinski.

"Thanks," said the security chief. Then he noticed Nancy, Bess, and George. "I thought I just got rid of you three. You sure *they're* not the ones who did it?" he asked Will.

"Nah," Will said. "They were in the room with

me when it happened. Besides, like I said, I already know who did it and who messed up the room next door. It was Sally Belmont."

"Either her or one of you other crazy mystery people," said Sherbinski. "It gets worse and worse every year. You know, the Chelsea Towers Hotel offered me a job and I'm thinking of taking it. At least they don't have a mystery convention every year."

"I hope you do a better job at the Chelsea Towers than you're doing here," said Nancy. "I know it must be hard for you with all those false alarms. But you can't assume every one of them is fake. You have a duty to investigate."

"Is that so?" Sherbinski raised an eyebrow at Nancy. "And you think *you* have a duty to tell me how to do my job?"

"Of course not," Nancy replied. "But someone's life could be in danger."

"Yeah, well, *I* call the shots around here. Remember that," said Sherbinski. "But just to show you I'm right, I'll go through the motions."

"Thank you," said Nancy in a relieved tone.

Sherbinski paused by the still-open door and scratched at the red paint with a fingernail. Then he headed down the hallway. "I'll be back later," he called over his shoulder. Then they heard him mutter, "Crazy mystery people."

"Okay, Girl Scouts," Will said, ushering Nan-

25

cy, Bess, and George out the door. "You've done your good deed for the day. Now let the star take a nap. I'm wiped out."

"Probably from making up that really good headline," George said under her breath.

"We're leaving," said Nancy from the hallway. "But let me just ask you one more question. Why are you so sure Sally Belmont set this whole thing up?"

"I told you," said Will. "She thinks I'm more popular with the fans than she is. And she's right. So she's always trying to get free publicity. Why do you think she came to this convention in the first place?"

"You're here too," said George.

"I'm doing it because it's in my contract that I have to help publicize the show. I have to go wherever the show's producers and public relations people decide to send me. But the clause isn't in *Sally's* contract. She can do whatever publicity she wants. Her darling manager, Denise Ellingsen, took care of that. Denise Ellingsen takes care of everything."

"Where is Denise Ellingsen?" Nancy asked.

"She should be arriving any minute," Will said. "Along with my manager, if he *manages* to show up. But I can't wait to see the look on Denise's face when she sees what a cheap stunt her precious client pulled. She won't believe it."

Laughing to himself, Will closed the door.

"I'd like to see Denise Ellingsen too," Nancy said. "Let's find out if she's checked in yet. She can probably tell us a lot more about Sally Belmont."

The girls took the elevator back down to the lobby and padded silently across the thick, flowered carpet. The lobby had emptied out in the past few hours. The only people there were a maroon-uniformed hotel clerk and a man and a woman standing at the registration desk.

The man was in his midthirties, tall and broad-shouldered, with hollowed-out cheeks and silky, wispy blond hair. His companion was a pretty black woman. She wore a bright blue dress with a colorful scarf draped over one shoulder.

The two were arguing so loudly that Nancy, Bess, and George could hear them all the way across the lobby.

"Don't blame me because we had to sit in the smoking section!" the man yelled. "Those were the only seats they had left."

"We wouldn't have had to sit in the smoking section if you'd made the reservations two weeks ago when I told you to instead of waiting till the last minute!" the woman yelled back.

"Excuse me, Ms. Ellingsen," the clerk cut in, "but your room is ready now. If you'll just sign here . . ."

27

"That's her!" Nancy whispered. "Sally's manager."

"And I'll bet that guy is Will Leonard's manager," Bess said.

"Sounds like they don't get along any better than Sally Belmont and Will Leonard do," commented George.

"Let's catch her before she goes upstairs," Nancy said. She ran across the lobby, with Bess and George close behind. The girls were moving so quickly, they practically crashed into Denise Ellingsen.

"Why don't you watch where you're going?" Denise Ellingsen said irritably.

"We're really sorry, Ms. Ellingsen," said Nancy, "but we have to speak to you."

Denise Ellingsen took a step back. "How do you know who I am?"

"Will Leonard said you'd be arriving, and we overheard your name. But that's not the important thing. Sally Belmont's missing!"

The star's manager raised her eyebrows. "Missing? What do you mean, missing?"

"She invited us up to her room, and when we got there it was ransacked and there was a note saying she'd been kidnapped."

Denise Ellingsen gasped. "I can't believe it!"

"I can." The blond man smirked. He narrowed his blue eyes. "Sounds just like something she'd pull."

"That's exactly what Will Leonard said," said Bess.

"This is Will Leonard's manager, Peter Thornton," Ellingsen said shortly. "And I don't know your names."

Nancy introduced herself and her friends, then said, "Ms. Ellingsen, you know Sally. Do you really think she'd set up her own kidnapping just for the publicity?"

"Of course not," Ellingsen said. "Sally doesn't have to go to all that trouble. She's been a star since she was five years old."

Nancy suddenly remembered the blue contact lens she found in Sally's bathroom. "What color are her eyes?" she asked the star's manager.

"Blue, of course," said Denise Ellingsen impatiently. "Everyone in America knows that. Look, what does the color of Sally's eyes have to do with anything? If she's been kidnapped—"

"I have a real reason for asking," Nancy said quickly. "Is blue their *real* color?" Nancy asked. "She doesn't wear tinted contact lenses, does she?"

"Did you see her in *Under the Christmas Tree*?" Ellingsen asked. "That was her first picture, twenty-five years ago."

"I've seen it at least ten times," said Nancy. "They show it every year at Christmas."

"You remember the last scene in the movie?" asked Ellingsen.

Nancy remembered the movie so well she could practically turn on a projector in her head. Five-year-old Sally was crying because she finally got the puppy she always wanted. The camera moved in real close on her blue eyes, and her mother said, "Don't turn those beautiful blue eyes red."

"Of course!" said Nancy. "Her eyes really *are* blue because they didn't *have* tinted contacts back then!" Nancy took the glass with the blue contact lens out of her purse. "I found this in Sally's bathroom," she said. "I have a feeling this belongs to the kidnapper."

"You said the kidnapper left a note too?" Ellingsen asked anxiously.

Nancy took the note out of her purse and handed it over to Ellingsen. The girls waited while Ellingsen and Thornton read it.

"Well," Sally's manager said with a sigh, "it *does* sound a lot like a note that was featured in a recent 'Nightside' episode." She shook her head. "But I still can't believe Sally would have set up something like this."

Thornton didn't say anything.

"I think it would be a good idea if you—and Mr. Thornton—came up to see Sally's room," Nancy said quietly but firmly.

Denise Ellingsen nodded and immediately picked up her suitcase. It was made of expensive leather with the initials *HP* printed all over it.

"I *love* your bag," Bess said as they headed across the lobby. "Is that a *real* Henri Puissant?"

Ellingsen nodded.

"It must have cost a fortune," Bess said.

Ellingsen shrugged. "I'd rather pay more for quality."

"Me too," Bess said. "But usually I can't afford it."

For the first time Ellingsen smiled. "That's how I used to feel. But don't worry. If you want something badly enough, you'll figure out a way to get it."

Nancy looked back and noticed that Peter Thornton was lagging behind.

"Aren't you coming, Mr. Thornton?" Nancy asked.

Thornton hesitated and looked nervously around him.

"What's wrong, Peter?" Ellingsen asked.

Thornton coughed, then silently picked up his worn canvas bag and followed them to the elevator.

The door to Suite 1204 was still untouched, so Nancy led the group inside. She showed the manager the skidmarks that curved across the marble floor like two black gashes. Sally's bedroom was exactly as Nancy had left it, with chairs and tables overturned and Sally's silky clothes on the floor.

Ellingsen turned to Peter Thornton. "You still think Sally did this all by herself?" she asked.

Thornton shook his head. He had a confused look on his face. "I'm not sure. I want to talk this over with Will."

"He's right next door," Nancy said. "He said he was going to take a nap."

The five trooped back through Sally's suite and down the hall to Will's room. "You're next!" was still scrawled on the door, each letter dripping like blood. Denise Ellingsen shivered when she saw it.

Peter Thornton knocked on Will's door. There was no answer.

"Knock a little louder," said Bess. "He's a heavy sleeper."

"How do you know?" asked George.

"I read it in the *National Tattler*," Bess said.

Thornton knocked again. There was still no answer.

"Will!" Thornton called, this time pounding on the door.

Nancy tried the doorknob. It turned easily. She opened the door. What they saw when they all stepped into the room made them gasp in horror.

"This is awful!" Denise Ellingsen cried.

"I don't believe it," Peter Thornton whispered, shaking his head.

"Oh, no, not again!" cried Bess.

Nancy led the way into the middle of the room. It was like an instant replay of what had happened next door. The dresser had been overturned, clothes were all over the floor, and, worst of all, Will Leonard was nowhere in sight!

4

Breakfast with a Suspect

Now both stars of "Nightside" were missing.

"I'm going to call Security," said Denise Ellingsen.

"No!" cried all three girls at the same time.

Denise and Peter exchanged a questioning look. Nancy tried to explain.

"We've already met with the chief of security twice in the past hour, and he didn't even believe there was a real kidnapping. He thinks we're playing a practical joke."

"I'm sure *I* can convince him it's no joke," said Ellingsen, picking up the phone receiver.

Seconds later she was put through to Ray Sherbinski. Nancy and her friends watched as Ellingsen become more and more frustrated as she tried to convince the security chief that the kidnappings were real and not a joke. Finally Ellingsen slammed down the receiver.

"That jerk doesn't believe me!" she said angrily.

"If you ask me," said George, "I think we'd have a lot better chance of finding Sally and Will if Nancy handles this herself."

Peter Thornton turned to Nancy and laughed. "You? You're just a teenage girl."

Bess walked up to him and rose to her full height of five feet four inches. Even so, Thornton towered over her. But Bess would not back down.

"You obviously don't know who you're dealing with," Bess said in her most adult voice. "Nancy Drew happens to be one of the most famous detectives in this country. She's solved dozens of crimes."

"It's true," George chimed in. "And we should know because we helped her. If you want proof, you can go over to Danner and Bishop's department store right down the street and talk to the owner, Carlin Fitzhugh. Nancy saved his store from disaster!"

George was referring to the case called *The Joker's Revenge*, when the girls had captured a mysterious "prankster" who had been trying to steal the store's furs and jewels.

Ellingsen looked from Nancy to Bess to George. Then she shrugged. "Tell you what. I'm going to call the police. But you can go ahead and do . . . whatever it is you detectives do."

"Thanks," said Nancy. "And I know exactly where to start."

Nancy headed straight for Will's bed. Pinned to the center of the bedspread, just as before, was a note. Nancy unpinned the note and read it aloud:

Now there are *two* on the dark side. Soon the lights will go out for good as Will and Sally go down in history. And I mean *down*.

Denise Ellingsen shuddered. "That sounds even worse than the last note."

"There's just one thing I don't understand about either note," Nancy said. "Whoever wrote them didn't ask for a ransom. That scares me even more because it sounds as if the person doesn't want money. The kidnapper just wants to hurt Sally and Will."

"Or worse," George said.

"There goes my fifteen percent," said Thornton.

Nancy knew Thornton was referring to the commission he made for being Will Leonard's manager. Thornton helped Will get parts on TV. In exchange he got to keep fifteen percent of whatever Will earned.

"Is money the only thing you're worried about?" Ellingsen said accusingly. "What about Will and Sally? Their lives may be in danger. I wouldn't be surprised if *you* arranged this kidnapping yourself."

"Me? I'm too disorganized to pull this off. *You're* the one who's so good at arranging things."

"I was on the plane when this whole thing happened," said Ellingsen.

"So was I," said Thornton.

"Then who did it?" Denise Ellingsen asked.

Nancy studied the two managers closely while they argued. It was possible that one of them could have done it. Either Ellingsen or Thornton could have set the whole thing up in advance, using an accomplice in Chicago. Traveling together would give them both a perfect alibi.

But what would either one of them gain if Sally and Will disappeared? They both depended on their stars for their incomes. No, Thornton and Ellingsen wouldn't have kidnapped the stars— unless they had a reason that was more important than money.

While Thornton and Ellingsen continued to argue, Nancy started to pick up clothes off the floor and place them on the bed. Will's clothes were much more casual than Sally's—lots of T-shirts and jeans and a leather jacket. It felt strange to be so close to the lives of two TV stars, to know exactly what they wore, without really knowing them at all.

Nancy looked back at Ellingsen and Thornton. The two managers were still arguing.

"Maybe Will's not paying you enough," Ellingsen was saying. "I know about all those debts you ran up buying expensive sports cars, designer clothes, that mansion in Bel-Air. I bet we'll see a ransom note from you real soon!"

"You don't know what you're talking about," Thornton yelled, "so why don't you keep your mouth shut?"

Nancy was beginning to get a headache from all the shouting. "Let's get out of here," she said to her friends.

Nancy, Bess, and George shut the door to Room 1203 behind them. They could still hear the yelling through the door. The managers were so busy arguing they hadn't even noticed the girls leaving.

"I think it's time to check out Eileen Braddock," Nancy said as they took the elevator back down to the lobby. "We still don't know what the connection is between her and Sally Belmont."

The elevator doors opened and Nancy led her friends across the lobby to a little alcove. In the alcove was a mahogany table with a courtesy phone.

38

"What are you going to do?" asked George. "Are you going to call Eileen Braddock?"

"Not exactly," said Nancy. "You're going to call her."

"Me?" George exclaimed. "I couldn't do that!"

"Why not?" Nancy asked.

"Well . . . she's famous! She's not going to want to talk to me."

"She might—if you say the right thing," Nancy said. "Tell her how you've read every single one of her books. She'll love that. Ask if you can meet her, and ask if you can bring a friend."

"All right. I'll give it a try," George said, picking up the receiver. The hotel operator connected George to Eileen Braddock's room. "I can't believe I'm doing this," George said as she waited for Eileen Braddock to answer the phone. Suddenly her eyes popped wide open.

"Uh . . . yes . . ." she said hoarsely. "You're Eileen Braddock! I know your voice because I heard you on a talk show once. That was when you were promoting *The Raven's Eye*. I just loved that book, especially the part where the woman knows the guy in the painting is watching her because the eyes move . . ."

George finally paused to listen.

Bess laughed. "She's even more nervous than I was when I met Will Leonard."

George spoke again. "You bet I'm a fan. I've

read all twenty-seven of your books, and I read *Death by Fear* four times." She gasped. *"You'd like to meet me?"* She shot Nancy a look, and Nancy gave her the thumbs-up sign.

"Uh . . . sure," George said. "Any time is fine. . . . Tomorrow? . . . Breakfast? . . . Great! We'd love to! Oh, uh, I have another friend who's also a big fan. Would it be all right if she came too? . . . Thanks. See you at eight!"

George hung up the phone.

"Perfect," Nancy said. "Except did you have to tell her I was a fan? I've never read any of her books. What do I do if she asks me a question?"

"No problem," George said. "I'll do most of the talking, and you can just fake it."

Nancy grinned. "I can just see Braddock's next title—'The Secret of the Phony Fan'!"

Early the next morning Nancy and George headed down the hallway of the tenth floor.

"Don't forget," Nancy said. "If she asks me a question about one of her books, you'll have to cover for me."

"Don't worry," said George confidently. "I'll handle everything."

The two stopped at Room 1027 and were about to knock when they heard a phone ring inside.

Nancy motioned to George to be quiet. She wanted to hear what Braddock had to say. It might be a clue to what was going on.

"You again?" they heard Braddock say in a loud voice. "I thought we agreed on an amount."

Nancy and George exchanged a look. Maybe there would be a ransom demand after all!

"No, no!" Braddock was shouting. "No one could pay that much. You'll never get a million. Better ask for less. . . . Listen, I'm expecting some people any minute. I can't stay on the phone."

Nancy heard the phone receiver slam down. She purposely waited a few moments so Braddock wouldn't think they'd overheard. Then she knocked.

The door opened and the girls found themselves standing face-to-face with Eileen Braddock, world-famous mystery writer.

Eileen Braddock was wearing a hot pink warmup suit that emphasized her heavyset figure. Her rumpled blond hair looked as if it hadn't been combed.

Braddock looked from one to the other questioningly. "Which one is . . .?"

Nancy waited for George to answer. But George just stood there, without saying a word. Nancy poked her in the ribs, but it didn't help. How could George clam up at a time like this?

"Well?" Braddock said impatiently. "I haven't got all day."

Nancy stepped forward. "I'm Nancy Drew," she said, "and this is George Fayne, whom you

41

spoke to yesterday. We're both really big fans of your work."

Nancy mentally crossed her fingers to make up for the lie.

Eileen Braddock smiled. "In that case, come in. I've had room service bring up breakfast. I can't spend too long chatting with you girls, though. I'm teaching a seminar on mystery writing, and it begins this morning at nine A.M. sharp."

Braddock led the girls to a small round table covered with a clean white tablecloth. The table was set with fine china and silver serving dishes. Nancy sniffed at the air. French toast, coffee, maple syrup—it smelled delicious.

"Have a seat," Braddock said.

The girls sat and helped themselves to breakfast.

"I always love hearing from my fans," Braddock said. "It helps me see what works in my books and what doesn't. I even get new ideas that way. So tell me—which of my books did you enjoy the most?"

Nancy looked over at George. George was staring at her plate, not even eating. She was still too nervous to talk. Nancy kicked her under the table, trying to get her to say something. George just stared back at her helplessly.

Nancy tried her best to remember the book George and Bess had talked about when the girls had first seen Eileen Braddock signing books at her booth. "Uh . . . I liked that real scary one . . . *Death by Murder*," she said.

"You mean *Death by Fear*," Braddock corrected her.

"Of course." Nancy laughed. "It's just that I'm so nervous meeting you, I can't think straight."

"That's silly," Braddock said, smiling. "There's nothing to be nervous about. I'm just a person like anybody else." She turned to George. "What about you? Which book was your favorite?"

George swallowed a big piece of French toast and finally found her voice. "I have a couple," she said. "*Death by Fear*, of course. But also *Mist of Cobwebs* and *Secrets of Autumn*." George pointed to a large cardboard display poster that was propped up against the wall. The poster was a painting of a beautiful young woman dressed in fashionable workout clothes. "I'm a big fan of Fifi Spinelli," she said. "She's so daring."

George and Eileen Braddock began to talk about some of Fifi's more adventurous cases. As they talked, Nancy looked around the room.

A compact computer sat on a desk with papers spread all around it. The unmade bed was also littered with papers. Nancy also noticed Braddock's bifocals sitting on top of the papers on the bed. Nancy turned her attention back to the table and peered closely at the author's eyes. They were a brilliant blue. Nancy wondered if that was Braddock's real eye color or if she was wearing tinted contact lenses.

". . . and the part where Fifi's crawling through the mud, wearing that designer suit and all the jewelry—that was great!" George was still talking about Fifi Spinelli. Nancy sighed. Now that her friend had finally started talking, it was going to be difficult to get her to stop.

"Excuse me," Nancy cut in, "but I couldn't help noticing you wear glasses. You don't also wear contact lenses, by any chance, do you?"

The author looked startled at the interruption. "As a matter of fact, I do. I'm wearing them now. But what does that have to do with anything?"

Nancy thought fast. "Well, I came up with this idea for one of your books, and I just wanted to run it by you."

Braddock looked intrigued. "What is it?"

"Well, this Fifi Spinelli character is so fashionable, I thought she'd be the type to wear contact lenses. And then I was thinking maybe she'd wear those *tinted* contact lenses. Is that the kind you have?"

Braddock frowned. "I really don't like personal questions, Ms. Drew. Either we talk about my books, or you can leave right now."

"I'm sorry," Nancy said. "I guess I've got blue contact lenses on the brain ever since I found one in Sally Belmont's bathroom."

"You know Sally Belmont?" Braddock asked.

"Not really," Nancy said. "That is, I never got a chance to know her. She's been kidnapped. And Will Leonard's been kidnapped too."

Braddock stared at Nancy in disbelief. "Kidnapped?" she said. "But I just spoke to Sally yesterday morning!"

"It happened yesterday afternoon," Nancy said. She paused for a moment. Then she said, "So you *do* know Sally Belmont. Do you know Will Leonard, too?"

"That's none of your business!" Braddock said, rising to her feet.

"I didn't mean to make you angry," Nancy said.

"Well, you did," the author snapped. "I don't have to put up with this. Get out of my room!"

"Why?" George asked. "What have we done?"

"I don't want to talk about it!" Braddock screamed. She marched to the door and yanked it open. The kindly mystery writer had suddenly turned into a very angry woman. "Now leave! Both of you!"

Silently Nancy and George stepped out into the hall. With a loud crash the door slammed shut behind them.

5

Shooting Star

"Whew!" said George. "You don't have to be a detective to see she was acting suspiciously. I wonder why she blew up like that when we mentioned Belmont and Leonard?"

"I don't know," said Nancy. "But we're going to find out. Let's go wake up Bess."

The girls returned to their darkened room and turned on the light. The room had two double beds and a cot so they could all stay together. Bess lay facedown on one of the double beds, one arm dangling on the floor.

"What a lazy slug," George said, shaking her head. She reached out a hand and shook her cousin's shoulder gently. "Come on, Bess, wake up."

"Unhhhhh," Bess moaned. "What time is it?"

"It's past eight-thirty," George told her. "We've got work to do."

Bess rolled over on her back but didn't open her eyes. "Can't we do it at a more civilized hour, like maybe late this afternoon?"

"Get up," Nancy said seriously. "I have an assignment for you."

At the tone in Nancy's voice, Bess immediately opened her eyes. "You found something?"

Nancy nodded. "Eileen Braddock freaked out when we mentioned Sally Belmont and Will Leonard, and she threw us out of her room. I want you to go downstairs and talk to the person who's running the 'Nightside' booth. See if you can pick up any gossip about the show—anything about Braddock and her connection with Belmont, and possibly Leonard."

Bess sat up and saluted, then hopped out of bed. "And what are you guys going to do?"

"We haven't ruled out Ellingsen and Thornton as possible suspects," Nancy said. "George, you and I should tail them today, see what they're up to. Why don't we all meet back in the coffee shop downstairs at noon?"

"Oh, good," Bess said. "At least I'll get to eat something. All this mystery solving makes me hungry."

"Everything makes you hungry," said George.

Nancy picked up Bess's travel alarm clock from

47

the night table. "Eight forty-eight," she said, reading the numbers. "The convention doesn't start again until nine." She turned to George. "Let's try the lobby. Maybe Ellingsen and Thornton will show up there first."

Nancy and George set up their stakeout on a big leather couch in the center of the lobby. From there they had a clear view of all the elevators and the big brass front doors of the hotel.

At nine forty-five Peter Thornton got out of an elevator and headed for the exit.

"Follow him," Nancy whispered. "I'll wait here for Ellingsen."

George jumped up and was out the door a few steps behind Peter Thornton.

At ten-fifteen Denise Ellingsen came out of another elevator. She was dressed in a red suit with gold buttons and was wearing a lot of gold necklaces. She didn't look like a kidnapper, but Nancy had learned long ago not to trust appearances.

Keeping her distance, Nancy followed Ellingsen out the door. Ellingsen turned right and walked briskly down the busy Chicago street. She seemed to be in a hurry. Could she be going to see the hostages? Or perhaps she and Peter Thornton had left the hotel separately to avert suspicion and were meeting somewhere outside the hotel. Maybe they didn't want to take the chance of being overheard if they met in one of their rooms.

Ellingsen paused to look in the window of a jewelry store. Then she picked up the pace again. As Nancy passed the jewelry store, she glanced into the window. The stuff in there looked expensive. Maybe Ellingsen *was* planning to leave a ransom note and was already figuring out how to spend the money. Maybe Ellingsen was the person who'd called Braddock asking about money. Maybe they were in this together!

Ellingsen arrived at the front door of Danner and Bishop, the exclusive department store Nancy had saved from the notorious "joker." Nancy followed Ellingsen through the familiar marble entrance, past the glass cases in the makeup department, and up the escalator to the shoe salon.

Nancy hid behind a display case and watched as Ellingsen tried on a dozen pairs of shoes. There was nothing too suspicious about that. Or was there? Wasn't it strange that Sally Belmont's manager was spending the morning shopping when she should have been doing everything in her power to find her client?

Finally Ellingsen pointed to six different boxes and pulled out a credit card. Then, armed with two large shopping bags, she headed back to the Buckingham Hotel.

When Nancy arrived at the coffee shop, Bess

and George were already sitting in a large booth. Three hamburgers, three diet sodas, and a large plate of french fries were on the table.

"Well?" Bess asked her. "What did you learn about Ellingsen?"

"That she's a shoe freak," Nancy said, picking up her burger. "That's all. What about Thornton?"

"He gave me the slip," George said. "I followed him out of the hotel, and he disappeared into a crowd of people. I walked for blocks, but I couldn't find him again."

"Great." Nancy sighed. "Then we're nowhere."

"Not nowhere," Bess said. "*I* found out something very interesting."

"You did?" Nancy sat up.

"I went to the 'Nightside' booth and talked to a woman who works on the show. This woman knows *everything* about the show. And she told me that Braddock wrote an episode of 'Nightside,' but the script was rejected!"

"That's probably what the inscription in *The Repeating Gunshot* refers to." Nancy munched a french fry thoughtfully.

"It could also explain why Braddock blew up," George said. "Maybe she's still angry they didn't take her script. And maybe she kidnapped Sally and Will for revenge."

"That's a possibility," said Nancy. "The inscription seemed friendly, but maybe it hides Braddock's true feelings." Nancy took a sip of soda. "But let's not forget that we have three other suspects: Thornton, Ellingsen, and Sherbinski."

"The security chief?" Bess asked.

"I'd be willing to bet that he still hasn't investigated the kidnapping," Nancy said. "I don't care what he says about 'going through the motions.' There's something strange about a security guard who doesn't do his job."

"But why would he want to kidnap Will and Sally?" Bess asked.

"He's always complaining about these mystery conventions," said George. "Maybe he wanted to ruin this year's convention so they won't have them anymore."

"Maybe," replied Nancy. "But we still need to check out all four of them."

Bess pulled a Mystery Lovers Convention flyer out of her purse. "We could do it tonight," she said. "It says here there's a Dress-Up Ball at eight o'clock in the Crystal Pavilion. You're supposed to come dressed as your favorite mystery character. I'm sure they'll all be there."

"Perfect," Nancy said. "If we disguise ourselves, we could talk to all of them again without their knowing it's us."

George took the flyer from Bess and studied it. "It also says Will and Sally are going to be there. I

51

wonder how they're going to handle that. And Matt Ziegler's going to be there too."

"Who's Matt Ziegler?" Nancy asked.

George rolled her eyes. "For a famous detective, you're not the biggest expert on mysteries. Matt Ziegler is president of Mystery Lovers of America and a TV scriptwriter for mystery shows. I'll bet he can tell us more about Braddock, Ellingsen, and Thornton."

As if he'd heard his name, Peter Thornton wandered into the coffee shop. He looked around nervously. Then he spotted the girls and came straight toward them.

"Glad I caught you," he said. "There's something we need to talk about."

Nancy, who was sitting by herself on one side of the booth, slid in to make room for Thornton.

Peter Thornton sat down. "Uh . . . you girls haven't told anybody about Sally and Will's disappearance yet, have you?"

"Just you and Denise," said Nancy. "And the security chief."

"But you haven't gone to the police?" Thornton asked.

Nancy shook her head. "Denise said she was going to call them."

"Well, she changed her mind," Thornton said. "I convinced her that we don't want anybody else to know—at least not yet."

"Why not?" Bess asked.

"They've been missing less than one day. And there's still a good possibility this is just a setup. Denise and I just want to avoid all the bad publicity until we know they're missing for real."

"I think we should spread the word they're missing," Nancy said. "You might think this kidnapping's a fake, but we don't."

"Yeah," said Bess. "If you really cared about their safety, you'd call the police right now."

"We *do* care," Thornton said. "We just don't want to alarm the producers of 'Nightside' unnecessarily. If they find out Sally and Will are gone, they'll ruin us! They don't like their stars to pull publicity stunts like this."

"But it's going to be awfully obvious Will and Sally are missing when they don't show up at the Dress-Up Ball tonight," Bess said.

"We're going to make an announcement saying they had to go visit a children's hospital instead."

"Oh, that's really touching," Bess said sarcastically. "You're not just covering this up, you're involving innocent children."

"Look," said Peter, "I know you think this sounds hard-hearted, but it's just for another day or so. Can't you give us that much time?"

Nancy studied Will Leonard's manager closely. Thornton was nervous, no doubt about it. He'd seemed nervous from the minute Nancy had seen him in the hotel lobby, and that was *before* she'd told him Sally was missing. That could mean he was the kidnapper. And if he was, of course he'd want to keep the press and the police away.

On the other hand, it was equally possible Thornton was nervous because his star client was missing and he really didn't want any bad publicity.

In either case, it wouldn't make much difference if they waited a little longer to alert the authorities. Nancy could still continue the investigation on her own. There might even be more danger to Will and Sally once the police got involved. The kidnapper might react violently and do something unpredictable.

Nancy decided to wait to tell the police. But she wasn't about to let Thornton know that. Better to keep him off-balance.

"I'm sorry," Nancy said, "but I think people should know what's going on. And nothing you say or do can change my mind."

Peter Thornton looked at her. Then, without another word, he got up and left the coffee shop.

After finishing their lunch and paying their bill, the girls went straight upstairs to the Grand Ballroom to buy what they needed for their costumes for the Dress-Up Ball.

At a few minutes before eight that evening, the girls crowded around the single bathroom mirror, putting the final touches to their costumes.

George, since she was the tallest, and also because she had brought a long raincoat, had decided to go as Sherlock Holmes. The Grand Ballroom, with all its mystery souvenirs, had provided the rest: the famous double-brimmed hat, a pipe, and a magnifying glass.

Bess had chosen to be Fifi Spinelli, the glamorous detective from Eileen Braddock's books, mostly because it was a great excuse to wear her most stylish clothes, high heels, and lots of jewelry.

Nancy was going as Miss Marple, the elderly lady detective from Agatha Christie's mystery books. The costume was perfect for that night because Nancy could completely hide her identity. Her face was powdered white with black lines drawn on to make her look old, and her hair was tucked up under a white wig. A knitted shawl completed the outfit.

George laughed. "If only Ned could see you now." She was talking about Nancy's longtime steady boyfriend, Ned Nickerson.

"I hope Ned doesn't mind going out with an older woman," Bess teased.

"All right, you two. It's eight o'clock," Nancy said. "Let's get downstairs to the Crystal Pavilion. I want to catch Matt Ziegler before the other fans do."

The girls were among the first to arrive. A band

was still setting up at the far end of the room. Waiters and waitresses in maroon uniforms were placing tiny hors d'oeuvres on silver trays.

A smiling, middle-aged man in a tuxedo stood just inside the door. His curly brown hair was beginning to gray, and he wore round, horn-rimmed glasses.

"Good evening, ladies," he said. "I'm Matt Ziegler."

"Mr. Ziegler, can we talk to you for a moment? In private?" Nancy said.

"Sure," said Ziegler. He led the girls away from the doorway to a corner of the room. "Is anything wrong?"

"I'm afraid there is," Nancy said. "Your two guest stars are missing."

Ziegler raised his eyebrows. "Sally Belmont and Will Leonard?" he asked. "But Peter Thornton said they were visiting a children's hospital."

"I know what he said," Nancy said. "But the truth is they've been missing since last night, and we think they've been kidnapped." Nancy went on to describe the ransacked rooms, the threatening notes, and Eileen Braddock's suspicious behavior.

"I'm not saying Braddock is definitely the kidnapper," Nancy continued, "but someone who works on 'Nightside' said she wrote a script for the show and it was rejected. So we think maybe Braddock has kidnapped Sally and Will for revenge. She certainly seemed angry enough to do something like that."

"I won't argue with you about Eileen's temper," Ziegler said. "I've known her for years, and I know how emotional she can get."

"How emotional?" Nancy asked. "Emotional enough to do something like this?"

"She's done some pretty crazy things," Ziegler admitted. "Like destroying manuscripts she's not happy with the day they're due at the publisher's. But I can't see her doing anything like this."

"Let me ask you just one question," Nancy said. "Does she wear blue contact lenses?"

"Why?" Ziegler asked in a puzzled voice.

"Because I found a blue contact lens in Sally Belmont's bathroom after she disappeared. It wasn't Sally's, so I'm assuming it's the kidnapper's."

"If there *was* a kidnapper," Ziegler said. "It could just be a stunt to boost interest in 'Nightside.'"

"That's what everybody says!" Bess cried in exasperation. "Why won't anybody believe the stars are really missing?"

"It *is* possible," Ziegler said. "But it's just as possible Sally and Will will turn up any minute. So don't worry about it, okay?"

Nancy couldn't believe what she was hearing. First Sherbinski thought the kidnapping was a setup, then Will Leonard, then Peter Thornton, and now Matt Ziegler. Never, in all the cases she'd solved, had so many people refused to believe a crime had been committed. That had to be more than a coincidence. Maybe Ziegler was in on this too! Nancy wondered how she'd be able to keep her eye on so many suspects.

"Look," Ziegler said, "since you girls are so interested in mysteries, how'd you like to watch the filming of a really *good* mystery show. It's much better than 'Nightside.' It's called 'Cop.'"

"Oh, I used to watch that all the time," said Bess. "But now it's on at the same time as 'Nightside,' so I don't watch it anymore."

"You and several million other people," Ziegler said, sighing. "Its ratings have dropped way down, but it's still a great show."

"I still watch it sometimes," said George. "I really like the star, Dan Redding."

"What's it about?" Nancy asked.

"It's about this really tough former policeman who was framed and kicked off the force, so now he's waging a one-man battle against crime," said Ziegler.

"I've seen the commercials," Bess said, reciting the slogan. "'He's a one-man police force. . . . He's . . . Cop.'"

Visiting the set with Matt Ziegler would give Nancy the chance to check him out further. "Sounds good," Nancy said. "We'd love to watch the filming."

"We've got a whole busload going over from the convention tomorrow morning at nine," Ziegler said. "Just meet us in front of the hotel."

The girls thanked Ziegler, who headed back to the door.

"What do we do now?" George asked.

"I don't know about you," Bess said, "but I know where *I'm* going." Nancy and George watched her totter away on her high heels toward a maroon-uniformed waiter holding a tray of little hot dogs.

"I should have known," George said, rolling her eyes.

Bess returned with a plate full of hot dogs. "Anybody want one?" she asked.

Nancy took one and popped it in her mouth. "Not bad," she said. "But try to keep your eye on the *door*, not the food, okay? We don't want to miss our suspects when they walk in."

"I can watch and eat at the same time," Bess said, sitting down in a nearby folding chair. "Besides, I need provisions. We don't know how long we're going to have to wait until they show up."

Four hours later the girls were still staring at the door. Not one of their suspects had shown up. Not Thornton, Ellingsen, Braddock, or Sherbinski.

"Where do you think they could be?" George asked. "We've been watching this door all night."

Nancy shrugged. "Beats me. Maybe Thornton and Ellingsen were embarrassed to come since their clients are missing. Maybe Sherbinski's shift is over or he's on duty somewhere else in the hotel. As for Braddock, who knows?"

"Maybe they heard the food was terrible," Bess said, clutching her stomach. "I feel sick."

"That's not from *what* you ate," George said. "It's how much."

"It's awfully coincidental that they *all* stayed away," Nancy said. "Could it mean they're all in this together?"

Bess yawned. "Or maybe they're all sleeping. It's after midnight."

Nancy rose from her chair. "Well, this was a total washout. Let's get some sleep ourselves. We've got to be up early tomorrow morning for the shoot."

The next morning Nancy, Bess, and George were on a big tour bus with twenty other conventioneers, heading for Chicago's Loop. It was called the Loop because of the elevated train that made a horseshoe loop through the area. The streets were narrow and dark in the shadow of the train. The buildings were big and old, with fancy carvings and statues on the outside.

The bus parked on one of the narrow side streets and everybody got out. Matt Ziegler was waiting for them on the sidewalk and led them to an open square at the end of the block. A statue of a strange-looking orange horse stood in the center of the square.

"This is where they're shooting the scene," Ziegler said.

Police barricades were set up all around the square. A motion picture camera was set up at one side, and crew members scurried around with walkie-talkies.

Ziegler led the group behind the barricades. Nancy, Bess, and George found a spot behind a barricade, but a little apart from the crowd. From where they were standing, they would have an unobstructed view of the filming.

"We'll be filming a shoot-out scene here in just a few minutes," Ziegler explained, "but don't worry. The bullets are blanks, so you're in no danger."

Everybody laughed.

"Before we start," said Ziegler, "I'd like you all to meet someone."

Ziegler waved in the direction of the camera, and Nancy noticed a tall man with broad shoulders sitting in a director's chair. He got up and approached them slowly.

"That's Dan Redding, the star of 'Cop,'" George whispered to Nancy.

Redding was in his late thirties, with sandy

61

hair, a rugged, handsome face, and steely blue eyes. He was big and muscular, like a football player.

"Hi, folks," he said simply. His voice was a deep monotone. "I hope you'll watch our show." Then he turned and walked away.

"He doesn't say much," said George. "Just like his character on the show."

"It's the next-to-last scene of the show," Ziegler explained. "Our hero is about to catch a hooded bank robber. Dan's character managed to infiltrate the gang of thieves, so he'll be wearing a hood too."

The director shouted something at Redding, and the star placed a hood over his head. He crouched down by the orange horse. Then he aimed his gun at a small building to the right of the girls. Nancy turned around and saw a hooded figure in the doorway of the building.

"That's the criminal," said Ziegler, "in case you hadn't guessed."

Someone yelled, "Action!" Redding jumped up and fired his gun toward the hooded "criminal."

Nancy heard a clang. She looked up and saw a bullet hole in a No Parking sign above her head. Nancy's heart jumped—the sign could have been *her!*

Nancy turned back to tell Redding his gun was loaded with real bullets, not blanks. But before she could open her mouth, she saw him whirl around and point the gun directly at her and her friends.

Wait! Nancy wanted to scream, but the word froze in her throat.

Redding pulled the trigger and fired again.

6

Room 1203, Revisited

Nancy leapt on top of Bess and George and knocked them down to the ground as several bullets whizzed over their heads.

"Cut!" yelled the director.

For a few seconds there wasn't a sound as the three girls lay on the ground in a heap.

Then everything happened at once. The other conventioneers crowded around them. Dan Redding towered over them. Crew members were shouting, and Matt Ziegler was running back and forth like a frightened puppy.

"Everyone back on the bus!" Ziegler shouted. "We're going back to the hotel!" He scurried toward the street where the bus was parked.

Reluctantly the crowd moved away from Nancy, Bess, and George. Mystery lovers all, none of them wanted to walk away from a real mystery: who had put real bullets in the gun? And why?

"Is anyone hurt?" Ziegler said, scurrying back toward them.

Nancy rolled over on the pavement and sat up. She bent and unbent her legs, felt her arms, then rose to her feet. "I'm still in one piece," she said. "How about you?" she asked her friends.

Bess and George stood up. Bess brushed some dirt off her skirt and pointed to some scrapes on her knees. "I haven't had those since I was eight," she said.

George held up her arms to show matching scrapes on her elbows. "It could have been a lot worse," she said.

"That's a relief," Ziegler said. Then he headed for the bus.

Dan Redding took a few steps toward them. He had taken off his hood. "I don't know what to say," he said. His voice was hoarse. "The eye-holes in that hood weren't made properly. I totally lost track of where I was aiming. I'm really sorry."

Nancy looked up at Dan Redding's handsome face. Were those tears in his blue eyes?

"I don't know what happened with that gun," he said, blinking. "But I know for sure it's never going to happen again. Nobody does this on my show. You hear that?" he shouted in the direction of the crew. "You costume and prop guys just lost your jobs!"

Redding turned and strode toward some crew members who were huddling by a trailer parked behind the statue. As Redding approached, they gathered even closer together.

Suddenly one man broke away from the huddle and raced away down the street. Before he turned the corner, Nancy realized who it was. It wasn't someone from the crew. It was Peter Thornton!

What was Will Leonard's manager doing on the set of "Cop"? He didn't have anything to do with the show. In fact, he worked for its biggest competitor. Was that the reason he was here? To check out the competition?

Maybe he planned to sabotage the show. It would be terrible for "Cop" if word got out that innocent people were almost killed on the set.

Or could this have something to do with the conversation they'd had yesterday in the coffee shop? Nancy had told Thornton he couldn't stop her from spreading news of the kidnapping— and she had already told Ziegler. Maybe the bullets were Thornton's way of keeping her quiet for good.

"I've got to check something out," Nancy said to her friends. She ran up to the corner Thornton had turned.

Nancy looked up the dark, empty street. There

66

weren't any cars or people because the street had been blocked off for filming. There wasn't any Peter Thornton, either. Just a bunch of little stores and coffee shops crowded together.

Just then Nancy was startled by a loud, screeching sound over her head. Nancy jumped. Then she laughed at herself when she realized it was just the squeaking wheels of the train running on the tracks above her.

Nancy turned back toward the square and rejoined her friends.

"Where'd you go?" asked Bess.

"I saw Peter Thornton running away from here," Nancy said. "I followed him, but he got away."

"What was Peter Thornton doing on the set of 'Cop'?" Bess wanted to know.

"That's exactly what I'd like to know," Nancy replied. "Maybe Ellingsen was right about him. Maybe he *is* after Will Leonard's money—and our blood!"

"You mean you don't think those bullets were an accident," said George.

"Think about it," Nancy said. "Nobody substitutes real bullets for blank ones unless there's a reason. And those bullets were coming right at us. Everyone else was standing farther away."

Bess shuddered. "You think Thornton did it?" she asked.

"Either him or one of our other suspects,"

replied Nancy. "Thornton ran away from the set—that makes him look pretty suspicious. Both he and Ellingsen work in the industry, so they could have friends who work on the show. Either one of them might have been able to get that gun. The same goes for Matt Ziegler. I'm not sure about Braddock and Sherbinski, but we can't rule out the possibility that they somehow managed to tamper with the gun."

"I guess the kidnapper thinks we're getting too close," said George.

"Which means time is running out," Nancy said. "I don't think the kidnapper is going to be satisfied with a few cuts and scrapes. Let's get back to the hotel and see what else we can find out before he or she strikes again."

The girls took a cab back to the hotel and pulled open the brass front doors. The lobby was once again humming with activity. Conventioneers wearing Mystery Lover T-shirts criss-crossed each other on their way to special events.

"Let's go back up to Will Leonard's room," Nancy said. "We left there so quickly when Ellingsen and Thornton were fighting that I never finished looking for clues."

Bess looked at her watch, then looked at George and fidgeted.

"What's the matter?" Nancy asked.

"Um . . ." Bess looked down at the floor.

"Well, George and I sort of signed up for a seminar on famous women detectives. And it started five minutes ago."

"But we really don't have to go," George said. "We'd much rather help you."

Nancy looked from one friend to the other. "It's okay," she said, smiling. "You've been missing all the fun at this convention. Go to the seminar, I'll check out Will's room, and I'll meet you in a couple of hours."

"You sure?" Bess asked.

"Positive," Nancy replied, heading for the elevators. "We don't need three people to search one room anyway. I'll see you later."

Once again Nancy found herself padding silently down the carpeted hallway of the twelfth floor. When she got to Will Leonard's room, she saw that the red painted words had been cleaned off the door, but she could still picture the ominous message in her mind: "You're next!"

Nancy shuddered. Then she noticed the door was open. That was lucky! Now she wouldn't have to figure out how to get inside.

Then Nancy paused. *Why* was the door open? Was somebody else inside?

Very slowly Nancy pushed open the door and looked in. The curtains were drawn and the lights were out. All Nancy could make out were the dim shapes of the bed and furniture still overturned on the floor.

Nancy shut the door quietly behind her and took a few steps into the room.

Suddenly a figure stepped out of the shadows and turned to face her. Even in the half-darkness, Nancy recognized the woman's shape: tall, heavyset, wearing baggy clothes.

It was Eileen Braddock!

7

Eileen Braddock Explains

"Looking for contact lenses, Ms. Drew?" said the mystery author.

Nancy took a deep breath. "Not exactly," she replied calmly. "But I didn't expect to find you in Will Leonard's room."

Eileen Braddock laughed nervously. "I guess you're wondering what I'm doing here," she said.

"There are a lot of things I'd like to know about you," replied Nancy.

"I'll be happy to tell you," said Braddock. "But do you mind if I turn on the light first?"

Eileen Braddock felt her way along the bed toward a light switch by the door. Nancy, fearful Braddock would make a run for it, also moved toward the door.

"Don't worry," said Braddock. "I won't try to escape." She fumbled for a switch, and one of the overturned lamps on the floor lit up. Its lampshade had fallen off, so the bare bulb cast a pool of light on the rug and formed eerie shadows on the ceiling.

Braddock turned back to Nancy. She was wearing her red Fifi sweatshirt and baggy red sweatpants. "I know it looks suspicious for me to be standing in Will Leonard's room in the dark," Braddock said. "But I could say the same thing of you."

"I'm not the one who blew up yesterday at the mention of the two stars of 'Nightside,'" Nancy responded. "What's your connection to the show? And how well do you know Will and Sally?"

Braddock sat on the edge of the bed. She ran one hand through her hair over and over again. "No matter how strange my behavior may seem, I don't know anything about the kidnappings."

"But you *do* know Sally Belmont," Nancy said. "You wrote an inscription to her in one of your books. 'Thanks for trying. Too bad it didn't work out.' What does that mean?"

Eileen Braddock looked surprised. "How do you know what I wrote to Sally?"

"I'll answer *your* questions later," Nancy said. "Right now, it's my turn."

Braddock sighed. "I've always been a fan of 'Nightside.' So I was very flattered last year when Sally Belmont herself called to tell me she was a fan of my novels. She wanted me to write an episode of 'Nightside.' She asked me to send the script to her and she would show it to the producers."

"Did you write it?" Nancy asked.

"Of course. That's a chance no writer would pass up. You can make a lot of money writing for television."

"So what happened?"

"Everybody loved my script. Except for one person. Will Leonard."

"Why didn't he like it?" Nancy asked.

"He thought I'd written too many lines for Sally and not enough for him. He refused to appear in that episode. So they never bought my script. I offered to revise it, but Leonard wouldn't even let me do that."

"Didn't Sally stand up for you?"

"No. That's what made me so mad. She's the one who asked me to write it in the first place, but she backed down right away. I felt as if she'd wasted my time. And I felt that Will was just being difficult to prove he was a star. I was very angry with both of them for a long time."

"How angry?" Nancy asked meaningfully.

Eileen Braddock continued running her hand

73

nervously through her hair until it stood up on end. Now Nancy understood why Braddock's hair always looked uncombed.

"Not angry enough to kidnap them, if that's what you mean," Braddock said. "Especially not Sally. After a while, I realized I couldn't blame her for Will's behavior. I even sent her an autographed copy of one of my books. And when we got to the convention, Sally called to invite me to dinner. I accepted the invitation because I'd gotten over my anger."

"Then what are you doing in Will Leonard's room?" Nancy asked pointedly.

Braddock smiled. "You can't write twenty-seven detective novels without learning something about solving mysteries. After you told me Will and Sally were missing, I decided to use what I'd learned to solve a *real* mystery."

Braddock seemed to have an answer for everything, but Nancy was still not convinced. Just yesterday the author had blown up at the mere mention of Sally and Will. Now she was trying to help save them. This turnaround was too quick to be believed.

Rather than challenge Braddock on this point, Nancy went ahead with her questioning. "One more thing," Nancy said. "When George and I were outside your room, we heard you on the phone with someone. You were telling them they couldn't get a million dollars for something."

Braddock glared at her. "You had no right to eavesdrop on my private conversation."

"We weren't eavesdropping," Nancy said. "We were standing outside your door because you invited us over."

"You still don't have a right to be so nosy," Braddock said huffily. "But since I want to clear my name, I'll tell you the truth. I was just giving a friend of mine some advice. She's a writer too, and she's about to sell a novel. She was asking me how much money she should ask for. It had nothing to do with Sally and Will."

Nancy studied Braddock's face in the eerie lamplight. The light bounced off the author's bifocals for a moment. Nancy noticed that behind her glasses, Braddock's eyes really were a brilliant blue. She wasn't wearing tinted blue contacts after all! Now Nancy was convinced that the blue contact lens she'd found belonged to the kidnapper. So that meant that Braddock was in the clear.

"Tell you what," Nancy said. "Why don't we search this room together?"

Braddock stood up and looked at Nancy suspiciously. "You've asked *me* a lot of questions," she said. "But you've never told me who *you* are. Why should I trust you? You lied to me yesterday when you came to visit. You pretended to be a fan. I'll bet you've never read a single one of my books."

"That's true," Nancy admitted.

"So who are you?" Braddock demanded. "Why do you care what happened to Will and Sally?"

"I'm an amateur detective," Nancy said. "You might say solving mysteries is my hobby."

"You and everyone else at this convention," Braddock said. "I'll bet you've never solved a real crime in your life."

"I've solved a couple," Nancy said modestly.

Braddock looked at her for a moment, frowning. "What did you say your name was again?"

"Nancy. Nancy Drew."

"Wait a minute." Braddock's face lit up, and she began to nod emphatically. "I *do* know about you! From my friend, Monica Crown. She raved about the way you cleared her daughter of a robbery charge."

Nancy smiled. "I was happy to help her. She's a wonderful woman and a terrific writer. That was a really exciting mystery to solve."

"Monica sent me an article about the case that was in the River Heights paper—the Case of the Disappearing Diamonds," Eileen Braddock said eagerly. "But it didn't have a picture of you."

"I'm just a detective," Nancy said. "Not a TV star."

"Detectives have fans too," said Braddock. "Just look at Fifi Spinelli!"

Nancy laughed. Then she said, "Well, maybe we'd better start looking for clues."

"I'll follow your lead," Braddock said.

Nancy strode over to the heavy drapes and pulled the cord to open them. Sunlight poured into the room. She blinked in the sudden light and turned back to face Braddock.

"I'll start by the door," she said.

"Right," said Braddock. "I'll check the bed."

Nancy got down on her hands and knees and began to search along the carpet by the door.

Eileen Braddock had disappeared behind one side of the bed. Nancy stood up to see what she was doing. Braddock sat up at the same moment. She was holding something in her hand.

"Look at this," the author said.

Nancy walked around behind the bed to see what the author was holding. It was a piece of gray cloth.

"Where was it?" Nancy asked.

"It was caught in the metal frame of the bed," Braddock said.

Nancy bent down to examine the cloth. It was made of a lightweight synthetic material. The gray color reminded Nancy of something, but she couldn't remember what. The cloth was only a few inches square, and it was frayed around the edges. "It looks like it was ripped off something else," Nancy said. "Maybe the kidnapper was wearing gray, there was a struggle, and the kidnapper's clothing was torn."

"That's exactly what Fifi Spinelli would have said," the author told her.

Just then they heard the door burst open. Nancy crouched even lower behind the bed and motioned Braddock to do the same. Nancy held her breath as she heard heavy footsteps tromp into the room, then stop. Quietly Nancy let out her breath and breathed in again. A familiar smell filled her nostrils—cigar smoke.

"Crazy mystery people," a voice muttered.

Nancy immediately recognized the raspy voice. It belonged to Security Chief Ray Sherbinski.

Nancy flattened herself against the floor. She didn't want Sherbinski to see her. Even if she explained that she and Braddock were investigating Will's disappearance, they could still get in a lot of trouble for being in Will's room.

But what was Sherbinski doing there? He hadn't wanted to investigate before. He didn't even believe the kidnappings were real. Why was he suddenly so interested in Will's room?

Nancy heard Sherbinski's heavy footsteps as he moved to another part of the room. Then she heard rustling papers. He must be looking for something, but what?

The footsteps approached again. From behind

the bed Nancy could see Sherbinski's heavy black shoes stop just inches away.

Please don't let him look down, Nancy thought. Her heart sank as first one plump gray knee, then the other, dropped down to the carpet. He was going to look under the bed! Now he'd find them for sure!

Nancy heard a wheezing cough. Sherbinski stood up with a grunt. He must have changed his mind. Kneeling down was probably too much effort for him. He *was* very heavy. Though Nancy was relieved, she couldn't help thinking Sherbinski wouldn't be much use against a real criminal.

Nancy heard more rustling, more footsteps, then a door slamming and the sound of a bolt turning in the lock.

The room was silent except for the sound of Braddock's and Nancy's breathing. Sherbinski was gone. Or was he? Slowly Nancy lifted her head above the edge of the bed. There was no sign of him. Nancy rose and walked around the bed to the door. She looked out through the peephole to see if anyone was in the hall. There was no one there. Gently she turned the doorknob to pull the door open. The door didn't move. Nancy pulled harder, but the door stayed shut.

Nancy jiggled the bolt above the doorknob, but it wouldn't budge.

Eileen Braddock rose stiffly from behind the bed. "You know," she joked, "it's easier writing mysteries than being in them." Then Braddock noticed the grim look on Nancy's face. "What's the matter?" she asked.

"The lock is jammed," Nancy said.

The author shrugged. "Don't worry, we'll just call Security and ask them to unlock the door."

"That *was* Security," Nancy responded. "And for all we know, he could be involved in the kidnapping. Then we'd be in even worse trouble than we are now."

"Oh." Braddock said. "Well, we'll just call the front desk and *they* can send someone."

"They'll send Security," Nancy said.

"Then what are we going to do?" Braddock fretted.

Nancy bit her lip. "I don't know." She sniffed the air—smoke again. Sherbinski couldn't still be in the room, could he?

This smoke smelled different, though. It was heavier than the other smoke. Sootier. Was Sherbinski smoking another brand of cigar? Nancy whirled around, expecting to see the man in the gray uniform. Instead, she saw something much worse.

Will Leonard's desk was ablaze. Smoke billowed through the room. The flames leaped across the desk to the drapes and began to spread upward.

Eileen Braddock started to cough, and Nancy banged on the door.

"Fire!" Nancy screamed. "Fire!"

But no one answered, and there was no way out!

8

Speeding Terror

Nancy's eyes were watering so much she could barely see. Grabbing a pillow from the bed, she fanned the air in front of her, trying to get to Will's desk where she had first seen the flames.

Through the smoke, Nancy could still make out a pile of papers on the desk, crackling and snapping as they rapidly turned to carbon. Nancy sprang across the room.

She yanked the heavy bedspread off Will's bed, sending clothes and pillows flying. She flung the bedspread over the desk, smothering the flames.

After making sure the fire was out on the desk, Nancy ran to the window. Braddock followed. Together, they tore down the smoking drapes, stamping out the beginning flames with their feet. The heat ate through the soles of their shoes, and sweat poured down their backs, but they ignored the discomfort. When they were sure every last lick of fire was out, Nancy kicked through the charred fabric lying on the blackened carpet. She felt something small and lumpy and nudged it out with the toe of her shoe. It was burnt and crispy, but Nancy could tell what it was—Sherbinski's cigar.

Nancy picked it up. Pushing a sweaty strand of hair behind her ear, she turned to face Eileen Braddock. "*Now* it's time to call Security," she said.

Eileen Braddock made the call. Moments later the bolt turned in the lock. Ray Sherbinski stood in the doorway of Will Leonard's room. "You again?" he asked, surprised.

Then Sherbinski noticed Nancy's soot-blackened face and all the damage in the room. "What happened here?" he asked accusingly, striding into the room. "We could have you kicked out of here for what you've just done."

"Correction," said Nancy. "For what *you've* just done."

"Me?" Sherbinski asked. "I just got here."

"And you just left here less than five minutes ago," Nancy said. "We saw you."

"What were you doing here?" Sherbinski asked. "You had no right to be in this room."

"I think the bigger question is what *you* were doing here," Nancy said. "It looks to me like you were here to set a fire. Tell me, Mr. Sherbinski. Did you do it because you knew we were in the room?"

"I didn't even see you!" Sherbinski blustered. "And I didn't start any fire."

Silently Nancy held out the blackened cigar. "Forget something?" she asked.

Sherbinski coughed and sputtered. "Where'd you find that?"

"On the floor where you left it," Nancy said.

Sherbinski started to sweat, dark patches spotting the light gray of his uniform. "I admit that's my cigar," Sherbinski said. "I'm no liar. But I swear to you the whole thing was an accident. I meant to put the cigar out, not set the room on fire."

"Whether it was an accident or not," Nancy said, "that still doesn't explain what you were doing in the room in the first place."

"I was investigating," Sherbinski said. "You're the one who told me the guy in this room was kidnapped."

"Are you sure you weren't really here to destroy evidence?" Nancy asked.

"I was here to do my job," Sherbinski insisted. "I told you I'd be back to investigate. And here I am."

"I thought you believed this whole thing was a

stunt set up by us 'crazy mystery people,'"
Nancy countered.

"I do," Sherbinski said. "But it *is* my job to
investigate, no matter what. You said so yourself.
Now, if you don't mind, I'd better call House-
keeping and get this mess cleaned up. And don't
worry. I won't mention any names."

"Good," Nancy said under her breath. "Because your name is on top of my list."

Sherbinski strode out the door, giving one last
nervous look into the room. As Nancy watched
the security chief leave, something about him
nagged at her brain—something familiar about
him.

Eileen Braddock held out the scrap of gray
cloth. "Do you want to hold on to this?" she
asked. "Now that I've seen how good you are at
handling detective work, I think *you* should keep
all the evidence."

As Nancy reached for the gray cloth, it suddenly hit her. The cloth was the same color as
Sherbinski's uniform! Either Sherbinski or some
other security person had struggled with Will
the day he was kidnapped. Nancy would have to
keep a close eye on Sherbinski from now on.

"I don't know about you," said Braddock, "but
I'm exhausted. I'm going back to my room for a
shower and a nap."

"I thought you wanted to help investigate,"
Nancy said.

85

The author smiled. "You don't need my help," she said. "I think if anyone can find Sally and Will, it's you. I'll just stick to writing." Hitching up her sooty sweatpants, Braddock headed for the elevators.

Nancy was feeling pretty tired herself, so she went back to her room. Not bothering to turn on the light, she collapsed on the bed. As she started to doze off, the door opened, and George and Bess entered the room, laughing.

"That female robot detective was the best," George was saying. "Not only did she think faster than anybody else, she was indestructible."

"Teflon coated." Bess giggled and turned on the light. Then she saw Nancy's sooty face and singed clothing.

"Whoa," said Bess. "Looks like Nancy could have used a little bit of that Teflon coating. What happened to you?"

Nancy opened her eyes. "There was a fire in Will Leonard's room," she said.

George and Bess ran to the bed. "Are you okay?" Bess asked anxiously. "Do you want us to call a doctor?"

"I'm fine," Nancy replied. "Just a little tired."

"How did it happen?" George asked.

Nancy told them about running into Eileen Braddock, discovering she didn't wear blue contact lenses, finding the gray cloth, hiding from Sherbinski, and smelling the deadly cigar.

"Sherbinski sounds pretty suspicious to me," George said. "He wouldn't investigate when you asked him to, then he suddenly appears in Will Leonard's room and sets it on fire! And that piece of gray cloth clinches it as far as I'm concerned. I say Sherbinski's your man."

"Me too," Bess agreed.

"I agree it *seems* to fit together," Nancy said. "But, except for Braddock, we haven't ruled out our other suspects. Like, what was Peter Thornton doing on the set of 'Cop' this morning when we got shot at? Why did he run away? And who put the bullets in the gun?"

"What about Matt Ziegler?" George said. "He was the one who invited us to the shoot today. Or should I say *shooting.*"

"He's another possibility," Nancy said. "And we still don't know enough about Denise Ellingsen to rule her out. There are still too many pieces missing."

Nancy was interrupted by the ringing phone. George reached to the bedside table to answer it.

"Hello?" George said. Her eyes grew wide. "Ten o'clock? We'll be there." She hung up the phone.

"Who was that?" Nancy raised herself up on one elbow.

"I don't know," George said. "It was a man, but his voice was muffled, like he was covering the mouthpiece with his hand. He said if we want to find Will and Sally, we should be in the lobby of the Fremont Art Gallery tomorrow at ten A.M."

"A man!" Bess exclaimed. "That rules out Ellingsen."

"Not necessarily," Nancy said. "More than one person might be involved."

"No matter who it is," said Bess, "I'm glad they're finally doing something. All this waiting has been murder."

George shuddered. "Did you have to use that word?"

At nine-thirty the next morning the girls stepped out the front doors of the Buckingham Hotel. Almost immediately a black-and-white taxi rounded the semicircular driveway and pulled up alongside them.

"Perfect timing," Nancy said, opening the back door for her friends. The three crowded into the backseat. "The Fremont Art Gallery," Nancy told the driver.

The driver just nodded, without turning around. The cab screeched around the corner and took off at high speed, heading for the highway that circled downtown Chicago.

"He's going a little fast," Bess said. "Maybe we should ask him to slow down."

"I'll say something," Nancy said.

Nancy couldn't see the driver's face because he was wearing a hat, but there was something about him that seemed familiar. As she tried to get a better look, he turned his face away from her.

"Excuse me," Nancy said, "but we were wondering if you could slow down?"

But instead of going slower, the driver put his foot on the accelerator. The car shot forward. Nancy checked the speedometer. They were moving at eighty miles an hour!

"Please stop!" Nancy screamed as the air whistled in through the windows.

The driver pulled onto an exit ramp, and the car began to slow down. But before Nancy could react, the driver opened the door and jumped out of the cab. Nancy heard a heavy thump, and the car speeded up again, going faster and faster.

In horror Nancy checked the speedometer. Seventy . . . eighty . . . ninety. The cab left the exit ramp and entered a main road, heading straight for oncoming traffic.

Nancy heard the horn shriek before she saw it. A schoolbus was barreling straight toward them, like a giant yellow cannonball.

"Oh, no!" Bess screamed. "Look out!"

9

Death Threat

Nancy dived over the front seat and grabbed the steering wheel. The taxi swerved wildly to the right. They missed the schoolbus by inches.

The schoolbus horn blared as the bus continued in the opposite direction. Nancy steadied the wheel.

There was a red light about half a mile ahead, and a line of cars in front of it. They had to stop now, or they were going to crash! Nancy slammed her foot on the brake, but the car didn't slow down.

Nancy saw what was wrong. There was a block of cement pressing against the accelerator pedal. No wonder the car wouldn't stop!

Nancy pushed at the cement block with her foot, but it was too heavy to move. She looked up again. They were fast approaching the line of stopped cars.

Nancy ducked to the floor and used all her strength to move the cement block. She dropped it with a thud on the brake pedal.

The cab lurched and spun around. The brakes squealed. Nancy grabbed the wheel and tried to straighten the car as it skidded to a halt. The car jumped the curb, barely missing a parking meter. Finally it came to a standstill.

Nancy took a few deep breaths. She looked over the back of her seat and saw two heaps on the floor in the back. "You okay?" Nancy asked them.

George lifted her head. "Are we still alive?" she asked.

Bess groaned. "From now on," she said, "I'm taking the bus."

"Let's get out of here," Nancy said. "I don't know about you, but I could use some air."

Shakily the girls climbed out of the cab. A small crowd had gathered around the car. One person asked the girls if they were all right. Nancy assured her that they were fine.

"We'll call the police later and tell them about the cab," Nancy said. "But right now we'd better focus on who just tried to kill us."

91

Still shaking, they walked along the city street.

"Who do you think he was?" Bess asked.

"I never got a look at his face," Nancy said, "but something about him seemed familiar. I think I've seen him before."

"Me too," George said. "I had this funny feeling that I knew his back. Does that sound weird?"

"How can you know someone's back?" Bess demanded.

George shrugged. "It was just a feeling."

Nancy said, "Now we know the whole gallery meeting was a setup. That guy called just to lure us into the cab so he could get rid of us!"

"I wonder where the driver is now," Bess said. "He could be lying at the side of the road somewhere."

"I doubt it," Nancy said. "He was out of the cab in a split second. I got the feeling he knew exactly what he was doing."

"You think he just got up and walked away?" Bess asked in disbelief.

Nancy nodded.

"Where do you think he went?" George asked.

"He might have gone back to the hotel. Which is where we'd better head."

"Do we have to?" Bess asked. "I mean, if that's where the guy is going, maybe we should head in the opposite direction."

Nancy turned to her friend. "It's okay if you don't want to go back," Nancy said. "In fact, if you want to go back to River Heights, I'll understand completely."

Bess put her hands on her hips. "Nancy Drew!" she cried. "I might not be the bravest person in the world, but I wouldn't back out in the middle of a case!"

Nancy smiled at her friend. "I know you wouldn't," Nancy said. "But we might find ourselves in even more danger before we're finished with this case."

"So what else is new?" George said, grinning.

"Well, I'm not going *anywhere*," Bess said firmly, "except back to the hotel. Where's the bus stop?"

Moments later the girls were sitting side by side on a city bus, heading back to the hotel.

As the bus neared the Buckingham Hotel, it stopped at a red light. Through the window Nancy saw a cab pull up to the entrance across the street. Denise Ellingsen got out. She was loaded down with shopping bags, this time from another big Chicago department store.

"That woman sure knows how to spend money," Nancy observed, pointing to Ellingsen. The three girls watched as a maroon-uniformed doorman opened the heavy brass doors and Ellingsen went inside.

"I wonder where she gets all her money from," George said. "Could she make it just from being Sally Belmont's manager?"

"It's possible," Nancy said. "Sally Belmont must make hundreds of thousands of dollars every year. And if Ellingsen gets a percentage of that, I guess she can buy all the shoes she wants."

"Maybe *I'll* be a manager." Bess sighed.

"But maybe Ellingsen got the money a different way," George said. "Maybe it's ransom money."

"There's just one problem," Nancy said. "No one's asked for or paid any ransom. So if she *is* the kidnapper, Denise Ellingsen is spending money she doesn't even have yet."

"Neat trick," Bess said.

The light turned green, and the bus pulled up to the bus stop. Nancy, Bess, and George got out and waited on the corner for the Walk light.

Suddenly Nancy pointed again. "In one door and out the other." she said.

Bess and George looked toward the side entrance of the hotel. Peter Thornton peered out from behind the door. First he looked one way, then the other. Then he quickly ran off into the parking lot, carrying a duffel bag.

"That was strange," George said.

"He seems to be doing a lot of running away lately," Nancy said. "You know, if *he* was the guy driving the cab, he would have had just enough

94

time to get back to the hotel, change his clothes, and sneak away again right about now."

The Walk light flashed, and the girls ran across the street and through the hotel entrance. Denise Ellingsen, still holding her shopping bags, was waiting by the front desk.

Behind the desk a clerk reached into one of the little mail cubicles. He pulled out an envelope and handed it to Ellingsen. She opened it, pulled out a piece of paper, and read it. Then Ellingsen gasped and dropped her shopping bags on the floor.

Nancy hurried across the lobby and picked up Ellingsen's shopping bags. "Is something wrong?" she asked.

Shaking, Ellingsen handed Nancy the piece of paper. "If you really are a detective," she said, "you'd better see this," she said. "Because I don't know what to do!"

Nancy took the piece of paper from Ellingsen. Stapled to the top corner was an instant photograph of Will Leonard and Sally Belmont holding up the morning edition of a Chicago newspaper. It had that day's date on it. The TV stars looked tired, and Will Leonard's clothes were even more wrinkled than usual. Other than that, they looked unharmed.

"They're still alive," Nancy said. "That's good, anyway."

Nancy quickly read the note. Now she understood why Ellingsen had dropped her shopping bags. The note said:

The Sands of Time are running out. Tune in to the next exciting episode of "Nightside" and watch the stars go out . . . as I execute them one by one.

10

A Major Setback

"You've got to do something," Ellingsen said desperately.

Nancy spoke calmly. "The kidnapper wouldn't have gone to all the trouble of sending us this photo and this note if Sally and Will were already dead."

"Then what's he waiting for?" Ellingsen demanded. "He still hasn't asked for ransom. What else could he want?"

"I don't know," said Nancy, "but we'll probably hear from him again before he does anything to hurt them."

"We can't just sit here and wait for him to strike," said Ellingsen. "We've got to find him!"

"That's exactly what we're planning to do,"

Nancy said. "And we've got another clue right here."

Nancy took a closer look at the photograph of Will and Sally. They were standing against a cement wall. There was a table in the picture, and on the table was a book, a red sweatshirt, and a digital clock.

Nancy squinted, trying to read the title on the book. She could just make out the three words: *Death by Fear.* It was the book written by Eileen Braddock. And, if Nancy was guessing correctly, the red sweatshirt was also Braddock's, the one that said "I'm a Fifi Fan" on it. The clock said 9:27 A.M.

"Look at this." Nancy showed the picture to Ellingsen. "The book on the table was written by Eileen Braddock, and the sweatshirt looks like the one we saw her wearing."

"I knew it!" Ellingsen exclaimed. "Ever since I found out she was going to be at this convention, I knew she'd cause trouble. She's had it in for the show ever since 'Nightside' rejected her script. She even threatened to sue Will and Sally!"

"That doesn't mean she'd try to kidnap them," Nancy said.

"Of course it was Braddock," Ellingsen said, pointing to the photo. "You've got proof staring you in the face."

Nancy put the photo back in the envelope with the threatening note. "I know the picture *seems* to point the finger at Eileen Braddock," Nancy said. "But we still don't have enough evidence. Why don't we go find Ms. Braddock and see what she's up to?"

"That's easy," said Bess. "She's teaching a mystery writers' workshop this morning. It started at nine A.M. and goes till noon. I was going to take it, but we haven't had time."

Nancy looked at her watch. It was eleven o'clock. She checked the bulletin board by the elevators. It said the workshop was being held in the Windsor Salon, on the second floor.

The double doors to the Windsor Salon were open. Nancy could see Eileen Braddock at the far end of the room standing behind a podium. As usual, the author was running her fingers through her hair, causing it to stand up on end. She wore a blue pullover sweater and blue slacks.

"You see?" Ellingsen said. "She's not wearing that tacky red sweatshirt. That *proves* she's the kidnapper."

"Not necessarily," Nancy said. "She just might have decided not to wear it—and she's not the only person on earth with that sweatshirt. They're being sold here at the convention."

The Windsor Salon was packed with people. A few of them were wearing red Fifi sweatshirts.

"Writing a mystery is like baking a cake," Eileen Braddock was saying into the microphone. "You've got to add the clues one layer at a time."

"What are you waiting for?" Ellingsen whispered in Nancy's ear. "Go ask her about the photograph!"

"Not so fast," Nancy said. "Before we break this up, I want to find out a couple of things."

Nancy slipped into the Windsor Salon and stood in the crowd near the back.

"Excuse me," she said to an elderly man on her right. On the jacket of his blazer he wore a button that said "I'm a Fifi fan."

"Have you been at this workshop all morning?" Nancy asked.

"I've been here since eight-thirty," he answered. "But it's been worth every minute. This woman really knows her stuff."

"Did Ms. Braddock leave the room at any point?" Nancy asked.

"Nope," the man answered. "She's been here the whole time. I didn't take my eyes off her for a second. Are you a mystery writer too?" the old man asked.

"No," Nancy answered.

"I am," he said. "I've never been published, but I've written thirty-six mystery novels. That's nine more than Eileen Braddock!"

Nancy smiled at him. "Good luck!" she said, slipping out to the hallway where Ellingsen and her friends waited.

"Well?" Ellingsen asked. "Are you going to call the police and have her arrested?"

"It would be a false arrest," Nancy said. "She's not the one who sent the photograph."

"How do you know?" Ellingsen asked.

"Because she's been here since nine o'clock this morning. The clock in the picture said nine twenty-seven. So she couldn't have been there when the picture was taken and she couldn't have sent it. If you don't believe me, ask the several hundred eyewitnesses who've been with her all morning."

"But what about the book and the sweatshirt?" Ellingsen asked.

"Think about it," Nancy replied. "If Braddock *were* the kidnapper, why would she go out of her way to put those things in the photograph? Those items would only incriminate her. Which leads me to believe someone *else* put those things there to frame Braddock."

Denise Ellingsen nodded. "I guess I see your point," she agreed reluctantly.

"So now what?" Bess asked. "We know Braddock isn't the kidnapper, but that still doesn't tell us who the kidnapper *is*."

"I'm going to call the police," Ellingsen said. "Now that I know the kidnapping is for real, I think it's time to show them the evidence."

Ellingsen stuffed the envelope with the photograph into her purse. "If you need me for anything, I'm in room Eight fifteen."

The girls went to their room too. Nancy turned

the key in the lock and pushed the door open.

As soon as Nancy turned on the light, she wanted to close the door again. Once again, a room had been ransacked—and this time it was theirs.

"My clothes!" Bess shrieked, running into the room. "I can't believe they did this," she cried as she waded through the dresses, pants, and blouses scattered all over the floor.

Nancy and George followed Bess inside. The mess was even worse than it had been in Will Leonard's or Sally Belmont's rooms. Both beds had been slashed open and mattress stuffing still floated through the air. The drapes had also been slashed and hung in ribbons over the window.

Nancy picked her way through the bedroom to the bathroom. The kidnapper had struck there too. The bathroom mirror had been shattered, its cracks forming a pattern like a giant spiderweb. Bottles of shampoo and perfume had been emptied all over the floor.

"Phew!" Nancy said, lifting her hand over her nose to filter the heavy odor of perfume. "That guy sure had a busy morning. First the cab ride, then trashing our room."

"If he's trying to scare us," said Bess, "he's sure doing a good job. I'm ready to check out right now."

"Isn't it enough that he's got Will and Sally?" George asked. "What does he want from us?"

"To stop us from finding him," Nancy said, kneeling by one of the beds and pulling out her suitcase. The suitcase, made of fabric, had also been slashed to shreds. "And I have a feeling he got the other thing he wanted too."

"What was that?" George asked.

Nancy stuck her hand through one of the tears in her suitcase and felt around. Just as she had feared, the suitcase was empty.

"He got the evidence," Nancy said. "The contact lens, the gray cloth, and the kidnap notes."

"Everything?" Bess asked.

"Everything," Nancy replied. "Our whole investigation is back to square one."

11

Too Many Questions, Too Few Answers

"That's it," said Bess, scooping clothes up from the floor and throwing them on the gutted bed. "I'm packing my bag—if I can find it."

"Is this it?" Nancy said, holding up a few tattered strips of canvas. Attached to one strip was a leather handle.

"Oh, no!" Bess moaned. "Do you know how much that suitcase cost me?"

"We know one thing," Nancy said. "He had a key. The door didn't show any signs of being forced open, and it was locked when we got here."

"Sherbinski!" Bess said. "He has a key to every room in this hotel."

"That's true," Nancy said. "But I'm beginning

104

to doubt whether Sherbinski could have been the cab driver. I didn't get a good look at him, but he didn't seem as old or as heavy as Sherbinski."

"And to jump out of the cab like that when it was going so fast, the guy would have had to be pretty swift," George added.

"That's right," Nancy agreed. "Sherbinski could barely kneel down to look under a bed. And Ellingsen was shopping. That leaves us with Thornton, at least until we find out more about Ziegler."

"We did see Thornton sneaking out of the hotel right before Denise Ellingsen got the note," Bess said. "And it was right after our delightful cab ride."

"The timing *was* right," Nancy agreed. "Let's go downstairs and see if the clerk at the front desk remembers who left the note."

Back in the lobby the girls studied the face of every clerk behind the desk.

"I wish I could remember what he looked like," Bess said. "But I wasn't paying attention."

"I think I remember a mustache," George said.

"And reddish blond hair," Nancy added. "I remember because it was the same color as mine."

"So where is he?" Bess asked. "I see a lot of maroon jackets but no mustache."

Nancy pointed to the front doors. "That's because he's not wearing his uniform."

A man in his midthirties with reddish blond hair and a mustache entered the hotel. He was wearing a baseball cap that said Dave. Whistling to himself, he headed for a door marked Employees Only.

Nancy, Bess, and George raced up to him.

"Excuse me," Nancy said. "But we need your help."

Dave turned around. "Hotel business?"

"Sort of," Nancy said.

Dave shrugged. "Well, technically I'm off duty, but I guess I can give you a few minutes."

"Thanks," Nancy said. "Weren't you on duty an hour ago?"

Dave smiled. "Good memory."

"Do you remember giving a note to an attractive black woman?" Nancy asked. "You might remember because the woman got very upset after she read it."

Dave pulled on the brim of his baseball cap. "You know," he said, "so many people pass through here it's hard to remember."

"Please try," Nancy said. "It was only an hour ago. The woman's name was Denise Ellingsen."

"Ellingsen . . ." Dave stroked his mustache. "Wait, yes, I do remember. The woman was carrying a lot of shopping bags, right? And she dropped them all over the floor?"

Nancy breathed a sigh of relief. "That's her," she said. "Now, do you remember who left her that note? It's very important that we find out. Someone's life could be in danger."

Dave smiled knowingly. "Oh, I get it. This is one of those 'Rent-a-Mystery' things for the convention, right?"

"It's no joke," Nancy said. "Please—do you remember anything about the person who left the note?"

Dave shook his head. "No," he said, "because I never *saw* the person who left it. I just turned around and found it lying on the counter."

"Oh," said Nancy, disappointed. "Well, maybe you can answer another question. In the past few days have you had any contact with another guest at the hotel named Peter Thornton? He's very tall and thin with sunken-in cheeks."

"Now, *him* I remember," Dave said. "He's some Hollywood guy, right? Works for that TV star. I took his reservation over the phone. I couldn't believe his nerve. He calls two days before the convention and expects to get the Presidential Suite. I told him 'Mister, I don't care *who* you work for, you have to call months in advance to get the Presidential Suite.' "

"Have you seen Peter Thornton at the hotel?" Nancy asked.

"Sure," Dave said. "I checked him out of here just this morning."

The girls looked at each other, their eyes wide with surprise.

"He's *gone?*" Bess asked Dave.

"He's history," Dave said. "Paid in full."

"Where did he go?" Nancy asked. "Did he leave any number where he could be reached?"

Dave shook his head. "I'm not sure *he* knew where he was going. It took the guy twenty minutes to find his credit card, plus he lost his room key. That guy's a mess. Now, if you don't mind, I'm on my break."

"Thanks for your help," Nancy said as Dave disappeared through the Employees Only door.

"It sounds like Peter Thornton was nervous," George said. "That would fit in perfectly with the cab ride and everything else that just happened."

"I agree," Nancy said, nodding. "It all seems to fit together."

"But we still don't know where he went," said Bess. "He could be anywhere."

"Not really," Nancy said. "If Thornton *is* the kidnapper, he's probably still in Chicago and probably close by. Our suspect's been in and out of this hotel for almost four days. Part of that time, he's been trying to scare us. He couldn't have done that if he was far away."

"So where do we look?" George asked.

"I think we should start right around the hotel," Nancy replied. "The last time we saw him he was heading across the parking lot."

"He went out the side door," George said. "That's right over there."

The three girls turned to leave but were distracted by two familiar figures rushing through the lobby from the elevator bank: Matt Ziegler and the star of 'Cop', Dan Redding.

The two made an odd-looking pair. Redding was so tall and broad shouldered, and Ziegler was so little and quick. The star had an urgent expression on his face as he strode rapidly across the lobby. Ziegler scampered after him like a puppy trying to keep up.

"I wonder where they're going in such a hurry," Bess said.

"Probably to shoot another exciting scene of 'Cop'" George said.

"Not looking like *that*," Bess said, pointing to Redding. "Look at him. He's wearing glasses, and his clothes are a mess. Stars only dress like that when they think no one is going to recognize them."

"Fat chance, with all the mystery fans walking around this place," said George. "Someone's bound to spot him."

Nancy studied Redding's face as the two men passed in front of her. Redding did look different from the first time she had seen him. Was it just the glasses? Or the frantic expression in his deep brown eyes? Whatever it was, he wasn't the cool, calm star from the morning before.

Redding and Ziegler continued toward the front door. Dan said something to Matt that

Nancy couldn't hear. Then he pulled open one of the heavy brass doors and rushed out into the afternoon.

There was something obviously going on with the two men. Nancy didn't know if it had anything to do with the disappearance of Sally and Will, but she wanted to find out.

"Mr. Ziegler," Nancy said, tapping him on the shoulder.

Matt Ziegler turned and gave Nancy a big smile. "I'm so happy you're all right!" he said. "I feel terrible about what happened yesterday. Eileen told me all about it."

"Thanks," Nancy said. "We were just wondering if something was wrong."

Ziegler's expression was grim. "I'm sorry I didn't believe you earlier. It turns out Sally Belmont and Will Leonard really *have* been kidnapped. The police were here just a few minutes ago. Someone sent Belmont's manager a threatening note saying he was going to execute both of them."

"We know," Nancy said. "We were with Denise Ellingsen when she got the note."

Matt Ziegler shook his head. "Will and Sally were supposed to host the Mystery Lovers Awards ceremony tomorrow night."

"I read about that in the flyer," Bess said. "Isn't it going to be held right next door at the old Atheneum Theater?"

110

Ziegler nodded. "That theater is rarely used these days, and only by special request. We had to pay a lot of money to book it for this ceremony. Unless we can find Sally and Will, the ceremony will be held without them."

"That's too bad," Nancy said. "I guess now you won't have a star for the program."

Ziegler smiled. "Wrong. That's what I was just talking to Dan Redding about. He's agreed to stand in for Will and Sally as our guest of honor. It's really not a stretch when you think about it. 'Cop' may not get the ratings 'Nightside' gets, but 'Cop' is actually a better show. And Redding's not just the star. He created it."

"It's still nice of Redding to fill in at the last minute," Bess said. "Considering he wasn't your first choice."

"That was Peter Thornton's doing," Ziegler said. "I don't know what Thornton said to Dan, but it must have done the trick."

"Peter Thornton?" Nancy asked. "He's Will Leonard's manager."

Ziegler shrugged. "I got the impression he was Dan Redding's manager. Anyway, I have a lot to do to prepare for tomorrow night. I hope you girls can make it."

"So . . ." Nancy mused as she watched Ziegler leave. "Peter Thornton manages Redding too. Funny he never mentioned it."

"I'm surprised he can manage two people,"

111

said Bess. "It seems as if he can't even manage his own life."

Just then Denise Ellingsen came running toward them, necklaces jangling. "I'm glad I found you," she said, panting for breath.

"Why?" asked Nancy. "Did you get another note?"

"No," said Sally Belmont's manager, gulping air. "But I found something that might lead us to Sally and Will!"

12

The Trail Gets Hot

"What did you find?" Nancy asked eagerly.

"This," said Ellingsen, holding up a cream-colored high-heeled pump.

"A shoe?" Bess asked. "How's that going to lead us to Sally and Will? Is it going to *walk* us to where they're hidden?"

"It's Sally's shoe," Ellingsen said. "I just found it outside."

"Are you sure it's Sally's shoe?" Nancy asked.

"Positive," Ellingsen replied. "I was with her the day she bought this pair."

"It looks pretty ordinary to me," Nancy said.

"But it's not," Ellingsen said. "First of all, it's a size eight triple A. Very few people have feet as narrow as Sally's. And second, it's got these black rubber taps on the heels. Sally puts them on all her shoes."

"That explains those black skid marks on the floor in Sally's entrance hall," Nancy said. "Where did you find the shoe?"

"I was walking past the stage entrance to the Atheneum Theater next door. And I saw these black skid marks on the sidewalk there too. Sally's shoe was lying right next to the skid marks."

"Then there's a good chance Sally and Will are being held inside the theater," Nancy said.

"And we saw Peter Thornton running in that direction just before you got that threatening note," George said.

"Thornton?" Ellingsen asked. "I can't say I'm surprised. He never was much of a manager. Maybe he figured he'd be better as a kidnapper."

"We still don't know Thornton *is* the kidnapper," Nancy said. "Let's go over to the theater and look around inside."

Denise Ellingsen led the girls out the side door of the hotel lobby. Outside, the sun was shining brightly, reflecting off the cars in the parking lot. The four squinted against the glare as they picked their way around the cars toward the back entrance of the theater.

"Here they are," said Ellingsen, pointing at the pair of skid marks on the sidewalk.

"They do look like the ones in Belmont's

room," Nancy said. "May I see that shoe for a minute?"

Ellingsen handed Nancy the cream-colored pump. Nancy stooped down and dug the heel into the pavement. Then she dragged it across the sidewalk a few inches. The heel left a black skid mark identical to the ones by the door.

Nancy stood up. "Sally and Will may be inside," she said excitedly. "Let's take a look."

Nancy tugged on the handle to the stage door. The heavy metal door didn't budge an inch. Nancy pulled again with all her weight, but the door stayed stubbornly shut.

"It's locked," she said. "Let's try the front."

The four hurried around the building. Nancy tried the front doors, but they were locked too. They continued around the building but found no other entrances. Finally they were back where they started.

"Well," said Nancy, pulling a Swiss army knife out of her purse, "it looks like we may need a little help."

"You don't really expect to pick the lock with *that*," Ellingsen said.

"Just watch her," George said. "She's real handy with that thing."

Nancy unfolded the nail file attachment and inserted it into the lock. Very gently, she jiggled it inside until she felt a spring pop. The bolt clicked.

"After you," Nancy said to the others, opening the metal door.

"Amazing," Denise Ellingsen said, shaking her head as they went inside.

Backstage, the theater was pitch black. The four paused inside, blinking, as their eyes got used to the dark. After a few moments they could make out the dim glow of several Emergency Exit signs.

"I can't see a thing," Bess complained. "How are we going to find them when I can't even find the nose on my face?"

Nancy felt around in her purse for her pocket flashlight and switched it on. "This will help a little," she said.

Nancy scanned right and left with the beam. To their right was a cement wall with a metal ladder attached to it. The ladder went all the way up to the flies above the stage. Craning her neck, Nancy shone the flashlight up at the flies, which were metal catwalks crisscrossing above the stage. Nancy knew the flies were used when stage crews hung scenery and created special effects like snow and rain.

To their left hung a narrow velvet curtain. A few feet in front of it was another curtain, with a third a few feet in front of that. Nancy recognized these as the wings of the stage. Nancy walked toward the curtains shining her beam ahead of her. Sure enough, she was on the stage.

116

It was empty, as far as she could tell. Identical velvet curtains hung on the other side.

Nancy walked out onto the stage and turned to face the blackness where she knew the audience should be.

"Hello!" she called, her voice echoing in the empty theater. She tried to scan the seats all the way to the back row with her flashlight, but the beam was too weak.

Nancy returned to her friends, and they scanned more of the backstage area. On one wall was a door marked Emergency Exit.

"Let's see where that exit leads," Nancy said, feeling her way forward. The others followed through the door, onto the landing of a staircase. Nancy shone the beam down the steps ahead of them as she took the stairs one at a time.

"I smell food," Bess said as they rounded another landing and headed down another flight.

"You always smell food," George said.

"I'm not imagining it," Bess said. "I smell french fries."

"Will you come off it?" George snapped. She was getting a little annoyed with Bess's one-track mind. How could her cousin think about food at a time like this?

"No, wait," Nancy said. "I smell it too."

They'd arrived at the bottom of the stairs. There was another emergency exit door. Nancy searched with the beam along the floor. She caught a glint of something lying on the floor by the door.

Moving closer, Nancy saw that the glint was the reflection of light in a foil wrapper. Next to the wrapper were two paper cups and a small white paper bag with a grease stain. The smell of french fries was stronger than ever.

Nancy leaned down to pick up the white paper bag. Sure enough, it was half-filled with french fries—and the french fries were still warm!

"Somebody else has been here," Nancy whispered. "And judging from the heat of these fries, they were here very recently. In fact, they're probably *still* here!"

At that very moment footsteps pounded on the floor above them.

"Let's go!" Nancy cried, rushing back up the stairs.

The four of them raced up the stairs to the top. The footsteps were louder and seemed to be coming from the direction of the stage. A woman's voice was shouting something, but Nancy couldn't make out the words.

"Where are they?" Ellingsen asked. "I wish we could find a light switch!"

Using her flashlight, Nancy led the others to the velvet curtains in the wings. Then she aimed the beam onto the stage. She could just make out two struggling figures.

"Sally!" Denise Ellingsen called. "Is that you?"

"Denise?" cried a woman's voice. "Help me!"

"It's her!" Ellingsen cried. "Where are they?"

Nancy tried to find the figures again with her flashlight beam, but the light suddenly flickered and died. The battery had been used up. Nancy was in the dark again.

Suddenly there was a burst of light as the backstage door opened. For a split second Nancy could see two figures silhouetted in the doorway, a man and a woman.

Nancy's eyes, unaccustomed to light, couldn't make out their features, but there was no mistaking Sally Belmont's long mane of glossy black hair. All Nancy could tell about the man was that he was tall and broad-shouldered. He was grabbing Sally roughly around the waist.

"Denise!" Sally called again. "Help me!"

The door closed again, plunging them once more in darkness.

"Hurry!" Ellingsen cried. "We've got to get outside."

Nancy ran toward the door. It took her several seconds to find the handle. She got the door open just in time to hear a screech of brakes.

Looking up, Nancy saw a car speed around the back of the theater and disappear down an alleyway.

"Where did they go?" Ellingsen asked as she, Bess, and George joined Nancy in the parking lot.

"We just missed them," Nancy said. "We were so close to finding Sally and Will, and now we've lost them!"

"But where was Will?" Denise asked anxiously. "The kidnapper had just Sally."

"My guess is the kidnapper has already moved Will someplace else—maybe to avoid suspicion, since he knows we're on his trail. We found him as he was coming back for Sally," replied Nancy. "The two questions are, where did he move them, and is he going to bring them back here?"

"This is terrible," George said. "We may never find Sally and Will now!"

"It's more terrible than you think," Nancy said.

"Why?" Denise Ellingsen asked. "How much worse could it be?"

"Because now that the kidnapper knows we're this close," said Nancy, "he might not wait any longer to keep his promise."

"You mean . . . what he said in his note?" Bess asked fearfully.

Nancy nodded grimly. "The Sands of Time may have just run out."

13

The Sands of Time

"Did you at least catch the make of the car or the license plate number?" Denise Ellingsen asked.

Nancy shook her head. "It was already halfway around the corner. I didn't even see what color the car was."

"I can't believe it!" Bess cried. "After all that, we didn't get a single clue."

"Wrong," said Nancy. "We actually got quite a few. Remember, even though we didn't see the kidnapper's face, we now know he's a tall man with broad shoulders."

"Sounds like our 'cabdriver,'" George said.

"Sounds like Peter Thornton," Ellingsen said.

"Could be," Nancy said. "Whoever he is, he seems to be working alone. So we can eliminate two more suspects. Matt Ziegler's too small to fit the physical description."

"And who's the other suspect?" Denise Ellingsen asked.

"You," Nancy said.

"Me?" Sally Belmont's manager raised shocked eyebrows. "How could you even *think* I might be the one? Sally and I are friends, not just business associates."

"When you're a detective, everyone's guilty until proven innocent," Nancy said. "And it wasn't until Sally asked you for help that I was sure you weren't involved."

"Well!" Ellingsen said huffily. "I'm glad my good name has been restored. But it's so typical that I have to suffer for Peter Thornton's mistakes."

"If Peter Thornton is the kidnapper," Nancy reminded her.

"Who else could it be?" Ellingsen asked. "We should call the police right now and have them put out an all-points bulletin. Maybe Thornton hasn't already left town."

"We can't do that," Nancy said. "We don't have any real evidence against him."

Denise Ellingsen sighed. "Well, if there's nothing else we can do, I'd better go back to my room to prepare my speech for tomorrow morning."

"What speech?" Nancy asked.

"There's going to be a special presentation on

mystery television shows for the convention. Originally, Will and Sally were going to talk about 'Nightside,' but now I'll have to stand in. I have to give a history of the program and talk about the clip we're going to show."

"Sounds interesting," Nancy said.

"Why don't you girls come as my guests?" Ellingsen said. "I'll make sure you get front-row seats."

The next morning at nine Nancy, Bess, and George entered the Crystal Pavilion. Rows and rows of velvet chairs filled the floor. At the far end of the room was a stage with a movie screen hanging at the back.

In front of the screen was a table and chairs. Nancy could see Denise seated at the table, along with Matt Ziegler and several others. Most of the chairs in the audience were already taken, but the girls pushed toward the front.

When they neared the stage, Denise waved and pointed to the front row. A long piece of masking tape ran along the backs of three chairs. "Reserved" was written on the tape in black ink.

As soon as the girls took their seats, a spotlight lit up Matt Ziegler. He stood up and took the microphone.

"Good morning, Mystery Lovers!" His voice boomed through the huge hall.

Everyone in the audience cheered wildly.

"We've got a great program for you, featuring all your favorite mystery programs from the dawn of television to the top series of today! We also have some very special guests with us—Elaine Cossack, star of 'The Gray Phantom'; Larry Greenberg, producer of 'Cop'; and Denise Ellingsen, representing the stars of 'Nightside'."

George turned to Nancy and Bess. "I guess he's not going to talk about the kidnapping."

"They're trying to keep this pretty quiet," Nancy whispered. "The police know, but they haven't told the press. Can you imagine what the *National Tattler* would do with a story like this?"

"'TV Stars Kidnapped by Martian UFO'?" offered Bess.

"I see what you mean," said George. "Publicity like that wouldn't help the investigation."

The lights dimmed, and Dan Redding's face appeared in a close-up on the screen. He stared straight ahead, his steely blue eyes catching glints of the sun. Synthesized music with a driving beat poured out through the giant speakers on either side of the stage. A deep announcer's voice intoned, "He's a one-man police force fighting a lone battle against crime . . . He's . . . Cop."

Nancy stared. There was something disturbing about Redding's face. But before she could figure out what, the film started rolling.

Dan Redding stood alone in a dark alley. Facing him was a gang of thugs. Single-handedly,

Redding knocked them out, one by one, until finally he was confronting the leader. The leader of the gang, a huge, muscular guy with a scar on his cheek, laughed menacingly and took a few steps toward Redding.

Redding gave the gang leader a karate kick, and the guy landed flat on his back. Then Redding placed a foot on the hoodlum's chest and pulled a walkie-talkie out of his pocket.

Nancy caught her breath. "This show looks great," she said to George and Bess. "I can't believe I never watched it before."

Using the walkie-talkie, Redding called the police station to have them send a squad car to arrest the gang leader.

The screen went dark, and the audience applauded.

"He's cuter than Will Leonard!" Bess said. "And I just love his monotone voice. He sounds so . . . cool."

"I'd forgotten how good that show was," George agreed.

The lights came on, then an older man with salt and pepper hair at the table stood up. "I'm Larry Greenberg, producer of 'Cop,'" he said. He pulled a pile of index cards out of the pocket of his tan jacket. "I'm not too good at memorizing speeches," he said, "so I'll keep this short. As you can see, 'Cop' is a great show. We may not be number one in the ratings anymore, but the quality is just as high as it ever was, and we owe it all to Dan Redding. He not only stars in the show, he created it. And I hope you'll do us a favor, and do yourselves a favor, by tuning in once again."

Larry Greenberg sat down, and Denise Ellingsen stood up.

"Does anyone out there know why 'Cop' isn't number one anymore?" she asked.

All together, everyone in the audience shouted out one word: "'Nightside'!"

"'Cop' *is* a good show," Denise Ellingsen said. "And when 'Nightside' first aired, two years ago, we were almost canceled because we were on against it. That's when 'Cop' was number one.

"But thanks to all you fans, 'Nightside' is now the highest-rated show in television history. And we owe it all to our writers, directors, and, most of all, to our stars, Will Leonard and Sally Belmont."

The audience cheered and stamped its feet.

"The clip you're about to see is from one of our most popular episodes, 'The Sands of Time.' I leave you now to Will and Sally."

Denise Ellingsen sat down. Two faces lit up the screen: Will Leonard with his three-day growth of beard and wrinkled suit, and Sally Belmont with her deep blue eyes and long black hair.

"Did you hear the title of that episode?" Nancy whispered to her friends.

"I didn't catch it," George said.

" 'The Sands of Time'!" Nancy said excitedly. "Remember the kidnap note? 'The Sands of Time are running out.' Maybe the kidnapper was making a reference to this episode!"

The film began to roll.

Sally and Will were in a beige sedan in hot pursuit of a black Italian sports car. The sports car screeched to a halt in a parking lot, and a huge man with a bald head jumped out of his car and ran toward the back door of a building. Sally and Will's car raced into the parking lot, parked, and Sally and Will followed the bald man through the back door.

It was dark inside the building, and Sally made a joke to her TV husband that no one could see how wrinkled his suit was. Suddenly the lights went on, and Will and Sally realized they were standing on the stage of an old theater.

Will and Sally looked out over all the empty seats, and Will made a joke that he'd always wanted to be a star but had hoped for a bigger audience. Suddenly a huge net fell on the two detectives, trapping them.

The net was hoisted forty feet in the air with the stars inside. It swung back and forth over the stage. Sally made a joke about a hammock.

The net holding Will and Sally was suspended from a rope hung over a metal railing. On the other side it was weighted down with sandbags, like a giant balance.

Then there was a shot of the bald-headed killer standing on the catwalk behind the metal railing. On one side of him the rope hung down, holding the net with Will and Sally. On the other side the rope hung down holding the sandbags. There was a closeup as the killer flicked open a cigarette lighter. Slowly he moved the lighter's flame to the rope that held the two sandbags.

"Oh, I get it," Bess whispered. "He's going to burn the rope. The sandbags will drop on one side, and Will and Sally will fall on the other side."

"And then we'll have a mush of Will and Sally," George said with a shudder. "I'm glad this is just a TV program."

The rope began to singe, turning black as it began to give way.

The screen went black.

As the lights came on, Nancy turned to her friends. "That scene in the theater looks uncomfortably familiar," she said.

"That's what I was thinking," said George. "You don't suppose the *real* kidnapper would—"

"He might if the stakes were high enough," Nancy said.

"What kind of stakes?" Bess asked.

"I can't say for sure just yet," Nancy said, "but I think it's time we paid another visit to the set of 'Cop.' I want to know more about what's at stake in the battle to be number one!"

14

It All Comes Together

As soon as the program was over, Nancy walked up onto the stage.

"Mr. Ziegler," she called. "I need to talk to you."

"Oh, hi," he said distractedly as he gathered up some papers on the table. "I'm sorry, but I really don't have time to talk. I've got to go directly from here to the Atheneum Theater to prepare for tonight."

"This will only take a minute," Nancy said. "I just need to know if 'Cop' is shooting today."

"As a matter of fact, it is," Ziegler said. "Why?"

"I'd like to visit the set again," Nancy said. "After seeing the clip here, I finally realized

129

what a great show it was, and I'd love to watch them film again."

Ziegler smiled. "You have good taste, but I don't think they want any visitors. The other day was a special exception because I know Dan."

Nancy thought quickly. "I understand they don't want to be disturbed," she said, "but after the accident the other day, I never really felt I got a good look."

Matt Ziegler's face took on an anxious expression. "Oh, yes," he said. "We're still terribly sorry about that. The prop and costume people were fired, by the way."

"What do you say?" Nancy asked. "Can we watch them shoot? We'd only stay a little while."

Nancy waited while Ziegler thought it out. She hoped he'd be afraid to say no. He knew Nancy could make trouble over the accident. The last thing he wanted was a lawsuit or bad publicity.

"Tell you what," Ziegler said. "I'll ask Larry Greenberg, the producer. I'm sure he'll say yes. They're shooting today at the Sears Tower. Why don't you and your friends head over there, and I'll get Larry to call and tell the director to expect you."

"Thanks," Nancy said. She hopped down off the stage and rejoined her friends.

"Well?" George asked.

"We're going to the Sears Tower," Nancy said. "Let's catch a cab."

"Couldn't we take a bus?" Bess asked. "It's just as fast."

"No, it isn't," Nancy said as the three girls took the elevator down to the lobby. "You're just afraid to get back in a cab again after what happened the other day."

"You're right. I am afraid," Bess said. She smiled weakly.

The elevator doors opened, and they crossed the lobby to the front door. Outside, Nancy waved down a cab as it pulled up to the entrance.

"Don't make me go in there," Bess begged.

George got in the taxi. Nancy followed, but Bess planted herself on the sidewalk.

"Come on," George said. "Don't be a chicken."

Bess stubbornly shook her head.

"C'mon, lady," growled the cab driver. "I haven't got all day."

"You know what they say," Nancy said. "When you fall off a horse, you have to get right back on."

"Good idea," Bess said. "I'll take a horse and meet you there."

Nancy got out of the cab, pulled Bess inside, and slammed the door. "The Sears Tower," she told the driver.

Bess curled up in a ball and kept her hands over her eyes.

"What's wrong with her?" the driver asked.

"Nothing," replied George. "But could you keep your speed to around twenty miles per hour?"

The cab crept over the Chicago River and slowly rounded the western edge of the Loop. The girls could clearly see the Sears Tower. One hundred ten stories tall, made of jet black steel, it rose in solitary glory above all the other buildings surrounding it. It looked like a sky-high telescope, broader on the bottom, and getting narrower and narrower near the top.

"Wow!" George breathed. "That's *big!*"

"Open your eyes, Bess," Nancy said. "This is really spectacular."

"I trust your judgment," Bess said, still covering her eyes.

The cab pulled up to the entrance. The Sears Tower rose so high they had to crane their necks to see the top. In the lobby, a clerk directed them to the lower level where they saw the camera, barricades, and the frenetic crew. Behind the barricades, two young actresses played out a scene in front of a store window.

Nancy, Bess, and George stepped off the escalator and headed for the barricades. The director approached them. He had a beard, aviator glasses, and a safari jacket.

"Girls!" he cried, opening his arms to hug them all. "Matt told me you'd be coming. I'm so happy you're all right."

"We're fine," Nancy said, looking past him. "But where's Dan Redding? Isn't the star supposed to be on the set?"

"He almost always is," the director said, "but this is one of the few scenes he isn't in."

"Oh," Nancy said, disappointed. "There was a question I wanted to ask him."

"Tell you what," the director said, leading the girls toward three empty director's chairs. "You make yourselves comfortable, and as soon as Dan gets here, I'll bring him right over."

"Where is he?" George asked as they sat down.

"That's a good question," the director said. "He actually *is* supposed to be here by now to prepare for the next sequence we'll be shooting."

A young man in a T-shirt and jeans, carrying a clipboard, overheard them and walked over. "Dan just called. He said he'd be a little late— something about preparing for tonight's ceremony."

The director rolled his eyes. "That's all we need. We're already a half-day behind with this episode. Do you know how much money that's going to cost us? We can't afford to lose any more time."

The young man shrugged and walked away.

"What's the next scene you're doing?" Nancy asked.

The director said, "It's one in which Dan jumps off the balcony and lands on the crooks."

"Don't you use stuntmen for that?" Nancy asked.

"No way," the director said. "Dan always does all his stunts. He used to be a stuntman."

Nancy stared at a button the director had pinned to his jacket. It was oversized, with the words "He's a one-man police force. . . . he's . . . 'Cop'" and a picture of Dan Redding's face. Dan Redding's steely blue eyes seemed to stare right back at Nancy.

Suddenly it hit her: those eyes. On the button and in the show, Dan's eyes were blue. But in the lobby, when he'd been wearing his glasses, his eyes were brown—which meant he wore blue contact lenses. Which meant the blue lens she'd found in Sally's bathroom could have been his!

Nancy thought about how tall Dan Redding was and how broad his shoulders were. Hadn't George said the cabdriver's back seemed familiar? Maybe it was familiar from having seen him on TV!

And if Dan Redding used to be a stuntman, he'd be able to jump out of a moving cab without getting hurt.

Scariest of all was the fact that Dan Redding had fired his gun straight at them while so many people looked on. You couldn't get more obvious than that. And he had set it up with the badly fitting hood so that no one would suspect a thing!

A cold chill crept down Nancy's back. She

leapt out of the director's chair and grabbed Bess and George by the arms. "We've got to get to the Atheneum Theater right away!" she cried.

"Why?" asked Bess. "What's wrong?"

"I should have realized it!" Nancy said. "All the clues were right there. I just didn't put them together."

"What are you talking about?" George asked.

"Dan Redding!" Nancy said. "It was him all along."

"Dan Redding?" George asked. "How do you know?"

"I'll explain it all in the cab," Nancy said. "If we don't get to the theater fast, Will and Sally will never film another episode of 'Nightside' again—because they'll be dead!"

15

The Sands Run Out

"Get us to the Atheneum Theater as fast as you can!" Nancy told the cab driver.

The driver stepped on the accelerator. The cab began to pick up speed, taking the girls back into the Loop.

"Oh, no! Not again!" Bess cried, sinking down into her seat.

"Please, Bess," Nancy pleaded. "We've got a lot more important things to worry about than the speed of this cab."

"So?" George asked. "What makes you think it was Dan Redding?"

Nancy went over the clues for Bess and George. "And the rest of it fits together too," Nancy added. "Remember the first note? The kidnapper said, 'Watch the rerun as history repeats itself.' The real clue was *rerun*."

"Rerun of what?" Bess asked, sitting up. Thinking about the clues was taking her mind off the cab ride.

"'The Sands of Time,'" Nancy said. "The episode we saw in the film clip. The killer had Sally and Will trapped in a theater, hanging from a net above the stage. And he was just about to burn the cord."

"You don't think Dan Redding would do that for real?" George asked fearfully.

"We already know he was holding them in the Atheneum Theater," Nancy said. "And the second note said, 'Will and Sally will go down in history. And I mean *down*.' I have a scary feeling he meant that literally."

"He couldn't let them drop!" Bess cried. "It's such a long way down."

"That's why I hope we're not too late," Nancy said as the cab screeched into the parking lot of the Atheneum Theater.

Nancy threw some money at the driver, and the girls barreled toward the side entrance.

"Locked," George said, tugging on the door handle.

Nancy dug into her purse for her Swiss army knife.

"Hurry, Nancy!" shouted Bess.

Before Nancy could unfold the nail file attachment, they heard a huge thud from inside the theater.

"Oh, no!" George cried. "We're too late!"

"You two go call the police," Nancy said, her nail file already inside the lock. "I'm going to try to find Sally and Will."

"Or what's left of them," Bess said grimly.

"Come on, Bess," George said, leading her cousin away.

Within seconds Nancy had the door open. Once again she stood in darkness. However, as she approached the stage, she saw that a few work lights were on. Their dim light cast eerie shadows on the stage.

Nancy crept a few steps forward to the velvet curtains hanging in the wings. Holding her breath, she scanned the stage for a sign of a net or two dead bodies.

Nancy let out her breath in relief. The stage was empty except for a giant sandbag. That must have been what had fallen earlier. So if Will and Sally were in the theater, they were still alive!

Nancy also wondered if Matt Ziegler was there. He'd said he was coming over to get the theater ready for the awards ceremony.

"Hello!" Nancy called. "Is anybody here? Mr. Ziegler?"

Nancy heard muffled sounds coming from above her head. She looked up and felt as if she *was* watching a rerun of "The Sands of Time."

Forty feet above the stage was a giant net. Knees and elbows poked out of holes in the heavy mesh, as well as long strands of silky black hair.

It was like the clip, but this time the kidnapper had added a chilling touch. One sandbag was labeled Will, the second was labeled Sally, and written on the third was Nightside.

"Sally? Will? Is that you?" she called up to the net. She heard muffled cries.

Nancy had to try to save Will and Sally. By the time the police got there, it could be too late.

Nancy turned to the backstage area. She remembered a ladder that would lead to the metal catwalks overhead. Sally and Will were hanging from the catwalk. Nancy felt around until her hand touched cold metal—a rung of the ladder. Nancy climbed until she reached the catwalk, forty feet in the air.

It was darker up there than on the stage below. Nancy gripped the handrail tightly as she inched toward the net in which Sally and Will were trapped.

"Sally? Will?" she called down to them. "Are you all right?"

Their answers were muffled. Redding had gagged them too.

Nancy moved closer until she was standing just beneath the rope that hung over the metal railing. She wasn't strong enough to lift the net up to the catwalk. What could she do?

A tiny flame suddenly appeared in the air before her, with an eye and a nose behind it. Startled, Nancy stepped back, nearly losing her balance.

"Watch your step, Ms. Drew," drawled a deep male voice. "It's a long way down."

It was Dan Redding. And he wasn't holding just a lighter. In his other hand he held a gun, and it was aimed straight at her.

She should have *known* Redding would be waiting. He wasn't about to leave with the job only half-done.

"They're waiting for you on the set of 'Cop,'" Nancy said, trying to sound casual.

Redding laughed. "There's a much more important show to do here," he said. "The final episode of 'Nightside.' And I mean final."

Nancy's mind raced. She decided to try flattery. "I hear you're incredibly talented. I knew you were the star of 'Cop,' but I never knew you created it too."

The flame flickered, and Nancy could see a grim smile behind it. "People think if you're a good-looking actor you can't think too," Redding said. "But all the years I was doing stunts and acting, I was watching those producers. I knew I could put on a better show than they could."

"Looks like you did," Nancy said. "I saw a clip of your show this morning. It was really great."

"It *is* great," Redding said with a touch of

sadness. "And for a while everyone else thought so too. Until *they* came along."

Nancy knew Redding meant Will and Sally.

"You can't blame them," Nancy said. "The audience decides which show they like better."

"How could anyone like their show better than mine? They're just a couple of clowns cracking jokes every two minutes. My show is serious drama."

"Isn't there room for both?" Nancy asked.

"The networks don't think so. They told us that unless our ratings improve, we're off the air. I can't let that happen."

Redding moved the flame to the side of the rope that held the sandbags. Nancy smelled something burning—Redding had singed the rope.

Nancy had to distract him before he burned it any further and the balance broke.

"Mr. Redding!" Nancy blurted before she knew what to say. "Uh . . . you may not know it, but I'm a detective myself."

"I figured," said Redding. "Or you wouldn't be standing forty feet in the air watching me do this. Of course, I wasn't prepared for an audience for this show. So after it's over, *you'll* have to be the grand finale."

"Tell me one thing before you go through with it," Nancy said. "How did you come up with such a complicated scheme?"

141

The flame moved away from the rope. Nancy sighed inwardly.

"Same way I write my show," Redding said. "I figured a mystery convention would be the perfect setting for a *real* murder mystery. I sent the security chief a memo telling him there was going to be a fake kidnapping of the 'Nightside' stars. I told him it was a publicity stunt and not to call the police."

"He sure believed you," Nancy said. "We had to twist his arm just to get him to look inside Sally's room. He kept calling us 'crazy mystery people.'"

Redding laughed. "That's exactly the way I would have written it."

"But *I* didn't believe it was a stunt," Nancy said. "I knew it was a real kidnapping."

"I never figured some kid would be on my trail," Redding said.

Keep talking, Nancy begged Dan Redding silently. Just keep talking.

"Anyway," Redding continued, "since I knew somebody would figure it out, I planted the phony clues in that photo to make people think Braddock did it."

"So the cement wall behind Sally and Will in the photo was a wall of the theater," Nancy said.

"Right," Redding replied with a grin.

"What about Peter Thornton?" Nancy asked.

142

"He's been running around like he's got something to hide."

Redding smiled. "He does, but it's nothing you'd care about. He's planning to drop Will as a client—"

"—and represent you instead," Nancy finished the sentence.

"How did you know?" Redding asked.

"Matt Ziegler told us."

Redding shrugged. "Anyway, that's why Thornton checked out of the hotel. He didn't want to face Will. Will was already looking for another manager, so Thornton decided to cut his losses and represent me instead."

Nancy tried to keep Redding talking.

"So you did this all by yourself?" Nancy said. "I guess it's like 'Cop.' You're a one-man show."

Redding smiled. "Right. You're as good at solving crimes as I am at making them up. How'd you figure it out, anyway?"

"From your notes," Nancy said. "You kept talking about reruns and 'The Sands of Time,' which I finally found out was an episode of 'Nightside.' Once I saw the film clip, I knew you were holding them in the theater. I also knew how you were planning to kill them."

"Not how I *was* planning," Redding said. "How I *am* planning." Redding flicked his lighter and leaned toward the sandbag rope.

"And I figured out it was you after I saw the real color of your eyes," she said quickly. "I found your blue contact lens on Sally's bathroom floor."

"Too bad about that," Redding said, pulling the lighter away from the rope. "It's one more reason I have to get rid of you too. I really am sorry about that."

Redding singed a little more of the rope. Below the catwalk, Will and Sally wriggled helplessly in the net.

"Wait!" Nancy cried. "There are still a few things I don't understand. What was that piece of gray cloth I found in Will's room?"

"Oh, that," Redding said. "I disguised myself as a security guard and got some maid to let me into Leonard's room."

"Where'd you get the uniform?" Nancy asked.

"Let's just say I 'borrowed' it from the Security department," Redding said.

"And you tore it in a fight with Will?" Nancy asked.

"You bet I did," Redding said, rubbing one arm. "I have to say one thing about the guy. He doesn't give up easily."

"And you were the one who put the bullets in the gun? And pretended your hood didn't fit right?"

"You bet."

"And you're the one who broke into our room and made that phony call about the gallery."

"It all comes together, doesn't it?" Redding asked. "By the way, I was the cabdriver too."

"I figured," Nancy said. "I guess you learned that stunt in your stuntman days."

Redding shook his head sadly. "It really is going to be a shame to kill you. You're a clever kid."

"You don't *have* to kill me," Nancy said. "And you don't have to kill Will or Sally either."

"I didn't plan to kill them," Redding said sadly. "They weren't supposed to know it was me. I wore a ski mask and disguised my voice. But today, when I brought them back to the theater, my mask slipped off. They saw me. So now I *have* to kill them."

Redding let the tiny flame stay near the rope for several seconds. The sandbags shifted slightly. Below them, the net began to sway.

"Yeah," said Redding almost to himself. "This is gonna work real nice. These two should fall hard. And then, Ms. Drew, it's your turn."

16

In the Spotlight

The smell of burning rope grew stronger. The rope had burned almost all the way through. Just a few strands held the sandbags up. And once the sandbags fell down on one side, Will and Sally would fall down on the other.

Desperately Nancy looked around for something, anything, to use against Redding. But there was nothing. In just a few seconds the rope would snap. Nancy could imagine the sickening thud as first the sandbags hit the ground, then Will and Sally.

"Bye bye, 'Nightside,'" Redding said. The final strand holding the sandbags started to give way.

Nancy leapt forward, grabbing the end of the

rope with one hand. She heard a huge thud beneath her as two sandbags hit the stage.

Nancy dangled from the rope, forty feet above the stage. She felt as though her arm were being pulled out of its socket. Across from her, Sally and Will dangled from the other end of the rope.

Nancy's weight was enough to keep all three of them from dropping to the ground.

"I'll get you for this!" Redding cried. He lunged toward Nancy.

Suddenly all the theater doors flew open at once. The lights burst on with sudden brilliance. An authoritative voice yelled, "Police! Freeze!"

A dozen police officers ran down the aisles toward the stage. Overhead Nancy heard a struggle as other officers grabbed Dan Redding. "Let me go!" he screamed in fury. "Let me go!"

Nancy knew there was no way Dan Redding would get free.

Bess and George ran from the wings to the stage below Nancy.

"You okay?" Bess called.

Nancy nodded weakly.

"Hold on," George said. "We're going to get you down from there."

Several police officers raced to the stage, dragging a heavy piece of blue plastic. The plastic was almost as big as the stage.

Gripping the rope tightly, Nancy strained to see what they were doing.

147

One officer pulled a plug. There was a loud hissing sound. The blue plastic rose, and Nancy realized what it was—a huge inflatable cushion to break her fall.

"Okay, Ms. Drew," a policewoman called to her from the catwalk. "We've got three officers up here holding the rope so the other two don't fall. We want you to let go of your end and fall onto the mattress. Do you think you can do that?"

"Just watch me," Nancy said faintly.

"At the count of three, Ms. Drew," the officer coached her. "One . . . two . . ."

Nancy didn't wait for the final count. She let go of the rope and closed her eyes.

It was like landing on a cushion of air. There was a burst of applause all around her. When she opened her eyes, she saw Bess and George hurry over. They lifted her from the air mattress.

As soon as Nancy and her friends were in the clear, the three officers on the catwalk lowered the net with Sally and Will.

Minutes later Nancy was being hugged by Bess, George, Will, Sally, and Denise Ellingsen. A handcuffed Dan Redding slumped in a seat in the audience, glowering at them.

A police officer pulled him to his feet. "Okay, Mr. Redding," said the officer. "It's down to the station house to book you for kidnapping and attempted murder."

"It's too bad too," another officer said. "I

really liked your show. You made me feel good about being a cop."

Nancy and the others watched the officers escort Redding out the stage door.

Then Bess said, "I'm so glad you're all right. When I saw you hanging up there, I could just imagine . . ."

"Enough, Bess," her cousin said. "Don't think about what could have happened. The important thing is that everybody's okay."

"Thanks to Nancy," Sally Belmont said, wiping a tear from her famous blue eyes. "For a couple of minutes up there, I thought it was all over for us. I don't know how I can ever pay you back."

"That goes double for me," Will Leonard said. "I know I was pretty obnoxious back at the hotel. I wouldn't have blamed you if you let me drop like a ton of bricks."

"No hard feelings," Nancy told him. "I'm sure you get people bothering you all the time for your autograph and everything."

"And that's another thing," Will said, turning to Bess. "I owe you one major autograph, with a personal dedication saying anything you want. In fact, I'll do better than that. How'd you girls like to come to Hollywood and visit us on the set of 'Nightside'? It's on me."

"That's a great idea," Sally said. "In fact, why don't you stay at my house? I've got ten bedrooms, so you can take your pick."

"And I'll lend them one of my sports cars," Will said.

"I'll pay for gas," Sally said.

"We'd love to come," Nancy said, smiling. "I can't help noticing, though, that you two are getting along a lot better than you were before."

"It's amazing how something like this can bring you together," Will agreed. "It made me realize what a strong person Sally is. And it made me realize I was too competitive with her. There's room for *two* stars on 'Nightside.'"

"And I realized Will isn't as arrogant as he seems," Sally added. "He just wasn't used to being a star. But he'll have to get used to it," she said, kissing him lightly on the cheek. "He's going to be a star for a long time."

That evening Matt Ziegler stood in front of the curtain of the Atheneum Theater, bathed in a giant spotlight.

His voice boomed over the microphone. "Good evening, ladies and gentlemen. I'd like to welcome you to the final event of this year's Mystery Lovers Convention—the annual Awards Ceremony. And here to introduce the awards is our honored guest, the star of 'Cop,' Mr. Dan Redding!"

The audience applauded, and the curtain opened—to reveal Will Leonard and Sally Belmont.

Flustered, Matt Ziegler took a step backward and almost fell over the podium. "Uh . . . ladies and gentlemen . . . I, uh, don't know what to say, I thought . . . I mean . . ."

Will calmly took the microphone from Ziegler and said, "Hi, everybody!"

The audience screamed and stomped their feet.

Will handed the microphone to Sally. "Thanks, Will," she said. Then she turned to the audience. "You haven't seen us at the convention since that first day. I don't know how much you know about what happened to us, but for a few days, our lives were in great danger." There was a hush over the theater as Sally told the audience about the kidnapping.

When she had finished, she handed the microphone back to Will, who said, "And if it weren't for one special person, there wouldn't be any more 'Nightside'—or any more *us*. She tracked down the kidnapper and saved our lives. So I'd like you all to welcome tonight's *real* honored guest—the real-life detective who saved us and our show—Ms. Nancy Drew!"

The applause was deafening. Nancy, in the wings with Bess, George, Denise Ellingsen, and Braddock, stood absolutely still.

The audience began to shout Nancy's name. "Nan-cy! Nan-cy! Nan-cy!"

"What's the matter?" Bess asked. "They're calling for you."

"I can't go out there," Nancy said.

"Why not?" George asked. "They love you."

"I'm a little afraid," Nancy admitted.

"Afraid?" Denise Ellingsen laughed in amazement. "After all you've been through?"

"What could you possibly be scared of?" Eileen Braddock asked. "You've faced fire, guns, a head-on collision. What's the problem?"

"You're never going to believe this," Nancy said, grinning widely. "But I've got stage fright!"

NANCY DREW® MYSTERY STORIES
By Carolyn Keene

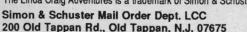